Books by Ernest Hemingway

THE COMPLETE SHORT STORIES

THE GARDEN OF EDEN

DATELINE: TORONTO

THE DANGEROUS SUMMER

SELECTED LETTERS

THE ENDURING HEMINGWAY

THE NICK ADAMS STORIES

ISLANDS IN THE STREAM

THE FIFTH COLUMN AND FOUR STORIES OF THE SPANISH CIVIL WAR

BY-LINE: ERNEST HEMINGWAY

A MOVEABLE FEAST

THREE NOVELS

THE SNOWS OF KILIMANJARO AND OTHER STORIES

THE HEMINGWAY READER

THE OLD MAN AND THE SEA

ACROSS THE RIVER AND INTO THE TREES

FOR WHOM THE BELL TOLLS

THE SHORT STORIES OF ERNEST HEMINGWAY

TO HAVE AND HAVE NOT

GREEN HILLS OF AFRICA

WINNER TAKE NOTHING

DEATH IN THE AFTERNOON

IN OUR TIME

A FAREWELL TO ARMS

MEN WITHOUT WOMEN

THE SUN ALSO RISES

THE TORRENTS OF SPRING

ERNEST HEMINGWAY

TO HAVE AND HAVE NOT

SCRIBNER PAPERBACK FICTION
PUBLISHED BY SIMON & SCHUSTER
NEW YORK LONDON TORONTO SYDNEY TOKYO SINGAPORE

SCRIBNER PAPERBACK FICTION
Simon & Schuster Inc.
Rockefeller Center
1230 Avenue of the Americas
New York, NY 10020

First Scribner Paperback Fiction edition 1996

SCRIBNER PAPERBACK FICTION and design are trademarks of
Macmillan Library Reference USA, Inc. under license by
Simon & Schuster, the publisher of this work.

Manufactured in the United States of America

20 19 18 17 16 15

Library of Congress Cataloging-in-Publication Data
    Hemingway, Ernest, 1899–1961.
        To have and have not.
        I. Title.
    |PS3515.E37T6   1987|
    813'.52   87-13254

ISBN 0-684-81898-1

PART ONE

HARRY MORGAN

(Spring)

CHAPTER ONE

YOU KNOW how it is there early in the morning in Havana with the bums still asleep against the walls of the buildings; before even the ice wagons come by with ice for the bars? Well, we came across the square from the dock to the Pearl of San Francisco Café to get coffee and there was only one beggar awake in the square and he was getting a drink out of the fountain. But when we got inside the café and sat down, there were the three of them waiting for us.

We sat down and one of them came over.

"Well," he said.

"I can't do it," I told him. "I'd like to do it as a favor. But I told you last night I couldn't."

"You can name your own price."

"It isn't that. I can't do it. That's all."

The two others had come over and they stood there looking sad. They were nice-looking fellows all right and I would have liked to have done them the favor.

"A thousand apiece," said the one who spoke good English.

"Don't make me feel bad," I told him. "I tell you true I can't do it."

"Afterwards, when things are changed, it would mean a good deal to you."

"I know it. I'm all for you. But I can't do it."

"Why not?"

"I make my living with the boat. If I lose her I lose my living."

"With the money you buy another boat."

"Not in jail."

They must have thought I just needed to be argued into it because the one kept on.

"You would have three thousand dollars and it could mean a great deal to you later. All this will not last, you know."

"Listen," I said. "I don't care who is president here. But I don't carry anything to the states that can talk."

"You mean we would talk?" one of them who hadn't spoke said. He was angry.

"I said anything that *can* talk."

"Do you think we are *lenguas largas*?"

"No."

"Do you know what a *lengua larga* is?"

"Yes. One with a long tongue."

"Do you know what we do with them?"

"Don't be tough with me," I said. "You propositioned me. I didn't offer you anything."

"Shut up, Pancho," the one who had done the talking before said to the angry one.

"He said we would talk," Pancho said.

"Listen," I said. "I told you I didn't carry anything that *can* talk. Sacked liquor can't talk. Demijohns can't talk. There's other things that can't talk. Men can talk."

"Can Chinamen talk?" Pancho said, pretty nasty.

"They can talk but I can't understand them," I told him.

"So you won't?"

"It's just like I told you last night. I can't."

"But you won't talk?" Pancho said.

The one thing that he hadn't understood right had made him nasty. I guess it was disappointment, too. I didn't even answer him.

"You're not a *lengua larga,* are you?" he asked, still nasty.

"I don't think so."

"What's that? A threat?"

"Listen," I told him. "Don't be so tough so early in the morning. I'm sure you've cut plenty people's throats. I haven't even had my coffee yet."

"So you're sure I've cut people's throats?"

"No," I said. "And I don't give a damn. Can't you do business without getting angry?"

"I am angry now," he said. "I would like to kill you."

"Oh, hell," I told him. "Don't talk so much."

"Come on, Pancho," the first one said. Then, to me, "I am very sorry. I wish you would take us."

"I'm sorry, too. But I can't."

The three of them started for the door, and I watched them go. They were good-looking young fellows, wore good clothes; none of them wore hats, and they looked like they had plenty of money. They talked plenty of money, anyway, and they spoke the kind of English Cubans with money speak.

Two of them looked like brothers and the other one, Pancho, was a little taller but the same sort of looking kid. You know, slim, good clothes, and shiny hair. I didn't figure he was as mean as he talked. I figured he was plenty nervous.

As they turned out of the door to the right, I saw a closed car come across the square toward them. The first thing a pane of glass went and the bullet smashed into the row of bottles on the showcase wall to the right. I heard the gun going and, bop, bop, bop, there were bottles smashing all along the wall.

I jumped behind the bar on the left side and could see looking over the edge. The car was stopped and there were two fellows crouched down by it. One had a Thompson gun and the other had a sawed-off automatic shotgun. The one with the Thompson gun was a nigger. The other had a chauffeur's white duster on.

One of the boys was spread out on the sidewalk, face down, just outside the big window that was smashed. The other two were behind one of the Tropical beer ice wagons that was stopped in front of the Cunard bar next door. One of the ice-wagon horses was down in the harness, kicking, and the other was plunging his head off.

One of the boys shot from the rear corner of the wagon and it ricocheted off the sidewalk. The nigger with the Tommy gun got his face almost into the street and gave the back of the wagon a burst from underneath and sure enough one came down, falling toward the sidewalk with his head above the curb. He flopped there, putting his hands over his head, and the chauffeur shot at him with the shotgun while the nigger put in a fresh pan; but it was a long shot. You could see the buckshot marks all over the sidewalk like silver splatters.

The other fellow pulled the one who was hit back by the legs to behind the wagon, and I saw the nigger getting his face down on the paving to give them another burst. Then I saw old Pancho come around the corner of the wagon and step into the lee of the horse that was still up. He stepped clear of the horse, his face white as a dirty sheet, and got the chauffeur with the big Luger he had; holding it in both hands to keep it steady. He shot twice over the nigger's head, coming on, and once low.

He hit a tire on the car because I saw dust blowing in a spurt on the street as the air came out, and at ten feet the nigger shot him in the belly with the Tommy gun, with what must have been the last shot in it because I saw him throw it down, and old Pancho sat down hard and went over forwards. He was trying to come up, still holding onto the Luger, only he couldn't get his head up, when the nigger took the shotgun that was lying against the wheel of the car by the chauffeur and blew the side of his head off. Some nigger.

I took a quick one out of the first bottle I saw open and I couldn't tell you yet what it was. The whole thing made me feel pretty bad. I slipped along behind the bar and out through the kitchen in back and all the way out. I went clean around the outside of the square and never even looked over toward the crowd there was coming fast in front of the café and went in through the gate and out onto the dock and got on board.

The fellow who had her chartered was on board waiting. I told him what had happened.

"Where's Eddy?" this fellow Johnson that had us chartered asked me.

"I never saw him after the shooting started."

"Do you suppose he was hit?"

"Hell, no. I tell you the only shots that came in the café were into the showcase. That was when the car was coming behind them. That was when they shot the first fellow right in front of the window. They came at an angle like this——"

"You seem awfully sure about it," he said.

"I was watching," I told him.

Then, as I looked up, I saw Eddy coming along

the dock looking taller and sloppier than ever. He walked with his joints all slung wrong.

"There he is."

Eddy looked pretty bad. He never looked too good early in the morning; but he looked pretty bad now.

"Where were you?" I asked him.

"On the floor."

"Did you see it?" Johnson asked him.

"Don't talk about it, Mr. Johnson," Eddy said to him. "It makes me sick to even think about it."

"You better have a drink," Johnson told him. Then he said to me, "Well, are we going out?"

"That's up to you."

"What sort of a day will it be?"

"Just about like yesterday. Maybe better."

"Let's get out, then."

"All right, as soon as the bait comes."

We'd had this bird out three weeks fishing the stream and I hadn't seen any of his money yet except one hundred dollars he gave me to pay the consul, and clear, and get some grub, and put gas in her before we came across. I was furnishing all the tackle and he had her chartered at thirty-five dollars a day. He slept at a hotel and came aboard every morning. Eddy got me the charter so I had to carry him. I was giving him four dollars a day.

"I've got to put gas in her," I told Johnson.

"All right."

"I'll need some money for that."

"How much?"

"It's twenty-eight cents a gallon. I ought to put in forty gallons anyway. That's eleven-twenty."

He got out fifteen dollars.

"Do you want to put the rest on the beer and the ice?" I asked him.

"That's fine," he said. "Just put it down against what I owe you."

I was thinking three weeks was a long time to let him go, but if he was good for it what difference was there? He should have paid every week anyway. But I've let them run a month and got the money. It was my fault but I was glad to see it run at first. It was only the last few days he made me nervous but I didn't want to say anything for fear of getting him plugged at me. If he was good for it, the longer he went the better.

"Have a bottle of beer?" he asked me, opening the box.

"No, thanks."

Just then this nigger we had getting bait comes down the dock and I told Eddy to get ready to cast her off.

The nigger came on board with the bait and we cast off and started out of the harbor, the nigger fixing on a couple of mackerel; passing the hook through their mouth, out the gills, slitting the side and then putting the hook through the other side and out, tying the mouth shut on the wire leader and tying the hook good so it couldn't slip and so the bait would troll smooth without spinning.

He's a real black nigger, smart and gloomy, with blue voodoo beads around his neck under his shirt, and an old straw hat. What he liked to do on board was sleep and read the papers. But he put on a nice bait and he was fast.

"Can't you put on a bait like that, captain?" Johnson asked me.

"Yes, sir."

"Why do you carry a nigger to do it?"

"When the big fish run you'll see," I told him.

"What's the idea?"

"The nigger can do it faster than I can."

"Can't Eddy do it?"

"No, sir."

"It seems an unnecessary expense to me." He'd been giving the nigger a dollar a day and the nigger had been on a rumba every night. I could see him getting sleepy already.

"He's necessary," I said.

By then we had passed the smacks with their fish cars anchored in front of Cabañas and the skiffs anchored fishing for mutton fish on the rock bottom by the Morro, and I headed her out where the Gulf made a dark line. Eddy put the two big teasers out and the nigger had baits on three rods.

The stream was in almost to soundings and as we

came toward the edge you could see her running nearly purple with regular whirlpools. There was a light east breeze coming up and we put up plenty of flying fish, those big ones with the black wings that look like the picture of Lindbergh crossing the Atlantic when they sail off.

Those big flying fish are the best sign there is. As far as you could see, there was that faded yellow gulfweed in small patches that means the main stream is well in and there were birds ahead working over a school of little tuna. You could see them jumping; just little ones weighing a couple of pounds apiece.

"Put out any time you want," I told Johnson.

He put on his belt and his harness and put out the big rod with the Hardy reel with six hundred yards of thirty-six thread. I looked back and his bait was trolling nice, just bouncing along on the swell, and the two teasers were diving and jumping. We were going just about the right speed and I headed her into the Stream.

"Keep the rod butt in the socket on the chair," I told him. "Then the rod won't be as heavy. Keep the drag off so you can slack to him when he hits. If one ever hits with the drag on he'll jerk you overboard."

Every day I'd have to tell him the same thing but I didn't mind that. One out of fifty parties you get know how to fish. Then when they do know, half the time they're goofy and want to use line that isn't strong enough to hold anything big.

"How does the day look?" he asked me.

"It couldn't be better," I told him. It was a pretty day all right.

I gave the nigger the wheel and told him to work along the edge of the Stream to the eastward and went back to where Johnson was sitting watching his bait bouncing along.

"Want me to put out another rod?" I asked him.

"I don't think so," he said. "I want to hook, fight, and land my fish myself."

"Good," I said. "Do you want Eddy to put it out and hand it to you if one strikes so you can hook him?"

"No," he said. "I prefer to have only one rod out."

"All right."

The nigger was still taking her out and I looked and saw he had seen a patch of flying fish burst out ahead and up the stream a little. Looking back, I could see Havana looking fine in the sun and a ship just coming out of the harbor past the Morro.

"I think you're going to have a chance to fight one today, Mr. Johnson," I told him.

"It's about time," he said. "How long have we been out?"

"Three weeks today."

"That's a long time to fish."

"They're a funny fish," I told him. "They aren't

here until they come. But when they come there's plenty of them. And they've always come. If they don't come now they're never coming. The moon is right. There's a good stream and we're going to have a good breeze."

"There were some small ones when we first came."

"Yes," I said. "Like I told you. The small ones thin out and stop before the big ones come."

"You party-boat captains always have the same line. Either it's too early or too late or the wind isn't right or the moon is wrong. But you take the money just the same."

"Well," I told him, "the hell of it is that it usually is too early or too late and plenty of time the wind is wrong. Then when you get a day that's perfect you're ashore without a party."

"But you think today's a good day?"

"Well," I told him, "I've had action enough for me already today. But I'd like to bet you're going to have plenty."

"I hope so," he said.

We settled down to troll. Eddy went forward and laid down. I was standing up watching for a tail to show. Every once in a while the nigger would doze off and I was watching him, too. I bet he had some nights.

"Would you mind getting me a bottle of beer, captain?" Johnson asked me.

"No, sir," I said, and I dug down in the ice to get him a cold one.

"Won't you have one?" he asked.

"No, sir," I said. "I'll wait till tonight."

I opened the bottle and was reaching it toward him when I saw this big brown buggar with a spear on him longer than your arm burst head and shoulders out of the water and smash at that mackerel. He looked as big around as a saw log.

"Slack it to him!" I yelled.

"He hasn't got it," Johnson said.

"Hold it, then."

He'd come up from deep down and missed it. I knew he'd turn and come for it again.

"Get ready to turn it loose to him the minute he grabs it."

Then I saw him coming from behind under water. You could see his fins out wide like purple wings and the purple stripes across the brown. He came on like a submarine and his top fin came out and you could see it slice the water. Then he came right behind the bait and his spear came out too, sort of wagging, clean out of water.

"Let it go into his mouth," I said. Johnson took his hand off the reel spool and it started to whiz and the old marlin turned and went down and I could see the whole length of him shine bright silver as he turned broadside and headed off fast toward shore.

"Put on a little drag," I said. "Not much."

He screwed down on the drag.

"Not too much," I said. I could see the line slant up. "Shut her down hard and sock him," I said. "You've got to sock him. He's going to jump anyway."

Johnson screwed the drag down and came back on the rod.

"Sock him!" I told him. "Stick it into him. Hit him half a dozen times."

He hit him pretty hard a couple of times more, and then the rod bent double and the reel commenced to screech and out he came, boom, in a long straight jump, shining silver in the sun and making a splash like throwing a horse off a cliff.

"Ease up on the drag," I told him.

"He's gone," said Johnson.

"The hell he is," I told him. "Ease up on the drag quick."

I could see the curve in the line and the next time he jumped he was astern and headed out to sea. Then he came out again and smashed the water white and I could see he was hooked in the side of the mouth. The stripes showed clear on him. He was a fine fish bright silver now, barred with purple, and as big around as a log.

"He's gone," Johnson said. The line was slack.

"Reel on him," I said. "He's hooked good. Put her ahead with all the machine!" I yelled to the nigger.

Then once, twice, he came out stiff as a post, the whole length of him jumping straight toward us, throwing the water high each time he landed. The line came taut and I saw he was headed inshore again and I could see he was turning.

"Now he'll make his run," I said. "If he hooks up I'll chase him. Keep your drag light. There's plenty of line."

The old marlin headed out to the nor'west like all the big ones go, and brother, did he hook up. He started jumping in those long lopes and every splash would be like a speed boat in a sea. We went after him, keeping him on the quarter once I'd made the turn. I had the wheel and I kept yelling to Johnson to keep his drag light and reel fast. All of a sudden I see his rod jerk and the line go slack. It wouldn't look slack unless you knew about it because of the pull of the belly of the line in the water. But I knew.

"He's gone," I told him. The fish was still jumping and he went on jumping until he was out of sight. He was a fine fish all right.

"I can still feel him pull," Johnson said.

"That's the weight of the line."

"I can hardly reel it. Maybe he's dead."

"Look at him," I said. "He's still jumping." You could see him out a half a mile, still throwing spouts of water.

I felt his drag. He had it screwed down tight. You couldn't pull out any line. It had to break.

"Didn't I tell you to keep your drag light?"

"But he kept taking out line."

"So what?"

"So I tightened it."

"Listen," I told him. "If you don't give them line when they hook up like that they break it. There isn't any line will hold them. When they want it you've got to give it to them. You have to keep a light drag. The market fishermen can't hold them tight when they do that even with a harpoon line. What we have to do is use the boat to chase them so they don't take it all when they make their run. After they make their run they'll sound and you can tighten up the drag and get it back."

"Then if it hadn't broken I would have caught him?"

"You'd have had a chance."

"He couldn't have kept that up, could he?"

"He can do plenty of other things. It isn't until after he's made his run that the fight starts."

"Well, let's catch one," he said.

"You have to reel that line in first," I told him.

We'd hooked that fish and lost him without waking Eddy up. Now old Eddy came back astern.

"What's the matter?" he said.

Eddy was a good man on a boat once, before he got to be a rummy, but he isn't any good now. I looked at him standing there tall and hollow-cheeked

with his mouth loose and that white stuff in the cor-
ners of his eyes and his hair all faded in the sun. I
knew he woke up dead for a drink.

"You'd better drink a bottle of beer," I told him.
He took one out of the box and drank it.

"Well, Mr. Johnson," he said, "I guess I better fin-
ish my nap. Much obliged for the beer, sir." Some
Eddy. The fish didn't make any difference to him.

Well, we hooked another one around noon and he
jumped off. You could see the hook go thirty feet in
the air when he threw it.

"What did I do wrong then?" Johnson asked.

"Nothing," I said. "He just threw it."

"Mr. Johnson," said Eddy, who'd waked up to
have another bottle of beer—"Mr. Johnson, you're
just unlucky. Now maybe you're lucky with women.
Mr. Johnson, what do you say we go out tonight?"
Then he went back and laid down again.

About four o'clock when we're coming back close
in to shore against the Stream; it going like a mill
race, us with the sun at our backs; the biggest black
marlin I ever saw in my life hit Johnson's bait. We'd
put out a feather squid and caught four of those little
tuna and the nigger put one on his hook for bait. It
trolled pretty heavy but it made a big splash in the
wake.

Johnson took the harness off the reel so he could
put the rod across his knees because his arms got tired

holding it in position all the time. Because his hands got tired holding the spool of the reel against the drag of the big bait, he screwed the drag down when I wasn't looking. I never knew he had it down. I didn't like to see him hold the rod that way but I hated to be crabbing at him all the time. Besides, with the drag off, line would go out so there wasn't any danger. But it was a sloppy way to fish.

I was at the wheel and was working the edge of the stream opposite that old cement factory where it makes deep so close in to shore and where it makes a sort of eddy where there is always lots of bait. Then I saw a splash like a depth bomb, and the sword, and eye, and open lower-jaw and huge purple-black head of a black marlin. The whole top fin was up out of water looking as high as a full-rigged ship, and the whole scythe tail was out as he smashed at that tuna. The bill was as big around as a baseball bat and slanted up, and as he grabbed the bait he sliced the ocean wide open. He was solid purple-black and he had an eye as big as a soup bowl. He was huge. I bet he'd go a thousand pounds.

I yelled to Johnson to let him have line but before I could say a word, I saw Johnson rise up in the air off the chair as though he was being derricked, and him holding just for a second onto that rod and the rod bending like a bow, and then the butt caught him in the belly and the whole works went overboard.

He'd screwed the drag tight, and when the fish

struck, it lifted Johnson right out of the chair and he couldn't hold it. He'd had the butt under one leg and the rod across his lap. If he'd had the harness on it would have taken him along, too.

I cut out the engine and went back to the stern. He was sitting there holding onto his belly where the rod butt had hit him.

"I guess that's enough for today," I said.

"What was it?" he said to me.

"Black marlin," I said.

"How did it happen?"

"You figure it out," I said. "The reel cost two hundred and fifty dollars. It costs more now. The rod cost me forty-five. There was a little under six hundred yards of thirty-six thread."

Just then Eddy slaps him on the back. "Mr. Johnson," he says, "you're just unlucky. You know I never saw that happen before in my life."

"Shut up, you rummy," I said to him.

"I tell you, Mr. Johnson," Eddy said, "that's the rarest occurrence I ever saw in my life."

"What would I do if I was hooked to a fish like that?" Johnson said.

"That's what you wanted to fight all by yourself," I told him. I was plenty sore.

"They're too big," Johnson said. "Why, it would just be punishment."

"Listen," I said. "A fish like that would kill you."

"They catch them."

"People who know how to fish catch them. But don't think they don't take punishment."

"I saw a picture of a girl who caught one."

"Sure," I said. "Still fishing. He swallowed the bait and they pulled his stomach out and he came to the top and died. I'm talking about trolling for them when they're hooked in the mouth."

"Well," said Johnson, "they're too big. If it isn't enjoyable, why do it?"

"That's right, Mr. Johnson," Eddy said. "If it isn't enjoyable, why do it? Listen, Mr. Johnson. You hit the nail on the head there. If it isn't enjoyable—why do it?"

I was still shaky from seeing that fish and feeling plenty sick about the tackle and I couldn't listen to them. I told the nigger to head her for the Morro. I didn't say anything to them and there they sat, Eddy in one of the chairs with a bottle of beer and Johnson with another.

"Captain," he said to me after a while, "could you make me a highball?"

I made him one without saying anything, and then I made myself a real one. I was thinking to myself that this Johnson had fished fifteen days, finally he hooks into a fish a fisherman would give a year to tie into, he loses him, he loses my heavy tackle, he makes a fool of himself and he sits there perfectly content, drinking with a rummy.

When we got in to the dock and the nigger was

standing there waiting, I said, "What about tomorrow?"

"I don't think so," Johnson said. "I'm about fed up
with this kind of fishing."

"You want to pay off the nigger?"

"How much do I owe him?"

"A dollar. You can give him a tip if you want."

So Johnson gave the nigger a dollar and two
Cuban twenty-cent pieces.

"What's this for?" the nigger asks me, showing the
coins.

"A tip," I told him in Spanish. "You're through.
He gives you that."

"Don't come tomorrow?"

"No."

The nigger gets his ball of twine he used for tying
baits and his dark glasses, puts on his straw hat and
goes without saying good-by. He was a nigger that
never thought much of any of us.

"When do you want to settle up, Mr. Johnson?" I
asked him.

"I'll go to the bank in the morning," Johnson said.
"We can settle up in the afternoon."

"Do you know how many days there are?"

"Fifteen."

"No. There's sixteen with today and a day each
way makes eighteen. Then there's the rod and reel
and the line from today."

"The tackle's your risk."

"No, sir. Not when you lose it that way."

"I've paid every day for the rent of it. It's your risk."

"No, sir," I said. "If a fish broke it and it wasn't your fault, that would be something else. You lost that whole outfit by carelessness."

"The fish pulled it out of my hands."

"Because you had the drag on and didn't have the rod in the socket."

"You have no business to charge for that."

"If you hired a car and ran it off a cliff, don't you think you'd have to pay for it?"

"Not if I was in it," Johnson said.

"That's pretty good, Mr. Johnson," Eddy said. "You see it, don't you, cap? If he was in it he'd be killed. So he wouldn't have to pay. That's a good one."

I didn't pay any attention to the rummy. "You owe two hundred and ninety-five dollars for that rod and reel and line," I told Johnson.

"Well, it's not right," he said. "But if that's the way you feel about it why not split the difference?"

"I can't replace it for under three hundred and sixty. I'm not charging you for the line. A fish like that could get all your line and it not be your fault. If there was any one here but a rummy they'd tell you how square I'm being with you. I know it seems like a lot of money but it was a lot of money when

I bought the tackle, too. You can't fish fish like that without the best tackle you can buy."

"Mr. Johnson, he says I'm a rummy. Maybe I am. But I tell you he's right. He's right and he's reasonable," Eddy told him.

"I don't want to make any difficulties," Johnson said finally. "I'll pay for it, even though I don't see it. That's eighteen days at thirty-five dollars and two ninety-five extra."

"You gave me a hundred," I told him. "I'll give you a list of what I spent and I'll deduct what grub there is left. What you bought for provisions going over and back."

"That's reasonable," Johnson said.

"Listen, Mr. Johnson," Eddy said. "If you knew the way they usually charge a stranger you'd know it was more than reasonable. Do you know what it is? It's exceptional. The Cap is treating you like you were his own mother."

"I'll go to the bank tomorrow and come down in the afternoon. Then I'll get the boat day after tomorrow."

"You can go back with us and save the boat fare."

"No," he said. "I'll save time with the boat."

"Well," I said. "What about a drink?"

"Fine," said Johnson. "No hard feelings now, are there?"

"No, sir," I told him. So the three of us sat there in the stern and drank a highball together.

The next day I worked around her all morning, changing the oil in her base and one thing and another. At noon I went uptown and ate at a Chink place where you get a good meal for forty cents, and then I bought some things to take home to my wife and our three girls. You know, perfume, a couple of fans and three of those high combs. When I finished I stopped in at Donovan's and had a beer and talked with the old man and then walked back to the San Francisco docks, stopping in at three or four places for a beer on the way. I bought Frankie a couple at the Cunard bar and I came on board feeling pretty good. When I came on board I had just forty cents left. Frankie came on board with me, and while we sat and waited for Johnson I drank a couple of cold ones out of the ice box with Frankie.

Eddy hadn't shown up all night or all day but I knew he would be around sooner or later, as soon as his credit ran out. Donovan told me he'd been in there the night before a little while with Johnson, and Eddy had been setting them up on credit. We waited and I began to wonder about Johnson not showing up. I'd left word at the dock for them to tell him to go on board and wait for me but they said he hadn't come. Still, I figured he had been out late and probably didn't get up till around noon. The banks were open until three-thirty. We saw the plane go out, and about five-thirty I was all over feeling good and was getting plenty worried.

At six o'clock I sent Frankie up to the hotel to see if Johnson was there. I still thought he might be out on a time or he might be there at the hotel feeling too bad to get up. I kept waiting and waiting until it was late. But I was getting plenty worried because he owed me eight hundred and twenty-five dollars.

Frankie was gone about a little over half an hour. When I saw him coming he was walking fast and shaking his head.

"He went on the plane," he said.

All right. There it was. The consulate was closed. I had forty cents, and, anyhow, the plane was in Miami by now. I couldn't even send a wire. Some Mr. Johnson, all right. It was my fault. I should have known better.

"Well," I said to Frankie, "we might as well have a cold one. Mr. Johnson bought them." There were three bottles of Tropical left.

Frankie felt as bad as I did. I don't know how he could but he seemed to. He just kept slapping me on the back and shaking his head.

So there it was. I was broke. I'd lost five hundred and thirty dollars of the charter, and tackle I couldn't replace for three hundred and fifty more. How some of that gang that hangs around the dock would be pleased at that, I thought. It certainly would make some Conchs happy. And the day before I turned down three thousand dollars to land three aliens on the Keys. Anywhere, just to get them out of the country.

All right, what was I going to do now? I couldn't bring in a load because you have to have money to buy the booze and besides there's no money in it any more. The town is flooded with it and there's nobody to buy it. But I was damned if I was going home broke and starve a summer in that town. Besides I've got a family. The clearance was paid when we came in. You usually pay the broker in advance and he enters you and clears you. Hell, I didn't even have enough money to put in gas. It was a hell of a note, all right. Some Mr. Johnson.

"I've got to carry something, Frankie," I said. "I've got to make some money."

"I'll see," said Frankie. He hangs around the water front and does odd jobs and is pretty deaf and drinks too much every night. But you never saw a fellow more loyal nor with a better heart. I've known him since I first started to run over there. He used to help me load plenty of times. Then when I quit handling stuff and went party-boating and broke out this swordfishing in Cuba I used to see him a lot around the dock and around the café. He seems dumb and he usually smiles instead of talking, but that's because he's deaf.

"You carry anything?" Frankie asked.

"Sure," I said. "I can't choose now."

"Anything?"

"Sure."

"I'll see," Frankie said. "Where will you be?"

"I'll be at the Perla," I told him. "I have to eat."

You can get a good meal at the Perla for twenty-five cents. Everything on the menu is a dime except soup, and that is a nickel. I walked as far as there with Frankie, and I went in and he went on. Before he went he shook me by the hand and clapped me on the back again.

"Don't worry," he said. "Me Frankie; much politics. Much business. Much drinking. No money. But big friend. Don't worry."

"So long, Frankie," I said. "Don't you worry either, boy."

CHAPTER TWO

I WENT in the Perla and sat down at a table. They had a new pane of glass in the window that had been shot up and the showcase was all fixed up. There were a lot of gallegos drinking at the bar, and some eating. One table was playing dominoes already. I had black bean soup and a beef stew with boiled potatoes for fifteen cents. A bottle of Hatuey beer brought it up to a quarter. When I spoke to the waiter about the shooting he wouldn't say anything. They were all plenty scared.

I finished the meal and sat back and smoked a cigarette and worried my head off. Then I saw Frankie coming in the door with some one behind him. Yellow stuff, I thought to myself. So it's yellow stuff.

"This is Mr. Sing," Frankie said, and smiled. He'd been pretty fast all right and he knew it.

"How do you do?" said Mr. Sing.

Mr. Sing was about the smoothest-looking thing I'd ever seen. He was a Chink all right, but he talked like an Englishman and he was dressed in a white suit with a silk shirt and black tie and one of those hundred-and-twenty-five-dollar Panama hats.

"You will have some coffee?" he asked me.

"If you do."

"Thank you," said Mr. Sing. "We are quite alone here?"

"Except for everybody in the café," I told him.

"That is all right," Mr. Sing said. "You have a boat?"

"Thirty-eight feet," I said. "Hundred horse Kermath."

"Ah," said Mr. Sing. "I had imagined it was something bigger."

"It can carry two hundred and sixty-five cases without being loaded."

"Would you care to charter it to me?"

"On what terms?"

"You need not go. I will provide a captain and a crew."

"No," I said. "I go on her wherever she goes."

"I see," said Mr. Sing. "Would you mind leaving us?" he said to Frankie. Frankie looked as interested as ever and smiled at him.

"He's deaf," I said. "He doesn't understand much English."

"I see," said Mr. Sing. "You speak Spanish. Tell him to rejoin us later."

I motioned to Frankie with my thumb. He got up and went over to the bar.

"You don't speak Spanish?" I said.

"Oh, yes," said Mr. Sing. "Now what are the circumstances that would—that have made you consider . . ."

"I'm broke."

"I see," said Mr. Sing. "Does the boat owe any money? Can she be libeled?"

"No."

"Quite so," Mr. Sing said. "How many of my unfortunate compatriots could your boat accommodate?"

"You mean carry?"

"That's it."

"How far?"

"A day's voyage."

"I don't know," I said. "She can take a dozen if they didn't have any baggage."

"They would not have baggage."

"Where do you want to carry them?"

"I'd leave that to you," Mr. Sing said.

"You mean where to land them?"

"You would embark them for the Tortugas where a schooner would pick them up."

"Listen," I said. "There's a lighthouse at the Tortugas on Loggerhead Key with a radio that works both ways."

"Quite," said Mr. Sing. "It would certainly be very silly to land them there."

"Then what?"

"I said you would embark them for there. That is what their passage calls for."

"Yes," I said.

"You would land them wherever your best judgment dictated."

"Will the schooner come to Tortugas to get them?"

"Of course not," said Mr. Sing. "How silly."

"How much are they worth a head?"

"Fifty dollars," said Mr. Sing.

"No."

"How would seventy-five do?"

"What do you get a head?"

"Oh, that's quite beside the point. You see, there are a great many facets, or you would say angles, to my issuing the tickets. It doesn't stop there."

"Yes," I said. "And what I'm supposed to do doesn't have to be paid for, either. Eh?"

"I see your point absolutely," said Mr. Sing. "Should we say a hundred dollars apiece?"

"Listen," I said. "Do you know how long I would go to jail if they pick me up on this?"

"Ten years," said Mr. Sing. "Ten years at least. But there is no reason to go to jail, my dear captain. You run only one risk—when you load your passengers. Everything else is left to your discretion."

"And if they come back on your hands?"

"That's quite simple. I would accuse you to them of having betrayed me. I will make a partial refund and ship them out again. They realize, of course, that it is a difficult voyage."

"What about me?"

"I suppose I should send some word to the consulate."

"I see."

"Twelve hundred dollars, Captain, is not to be despised at present."

"When would I get the money?"

"Two hundred when you agree and a thousand when you load."

"Suppose I went off with the two hundred?"

"I could do nothing, of course," he smiled. "But I know you wouldn't do such a thing, Captain."

"Have you got the two hundred with you?"

"Of course."

"Put it under the plate." He did.

"All right," I said. "I'll clear in the morning and pull out at dark. Now, where do we load?"

"How would Bacuranao be?"

"All right. Have you got it fixed?"

"Of course."

"Now, about the loading," I said. "You show two lights, one above the other, at the point. I'll come in when I see them. You come out in a boat and load from the boat. You come yourself and you bring the money. I won't take one on board until I have it."

"No," he said, "one-half when you start to load and the other when you are finished."

"All right," I said. "That's reasonable."

"So everything is understood?"

"I guess so," I said. "There's no baggage and no arms. No guns, knives, or razors; nothing. I have to know about that."

"Captain," said Mr. Sing, "have you no trust in me? Don't you see our interests are identical?"

"You'll make sure?"

"Please do not embarrass me," he said. "Do you not see how our interests coincide?"

"All right," I told him. "What time will you be there?"

"Before midnight."

"All right," I said. "I guess that's all."

"How do you want the money?"

"In hundreds is all right."

He stood up and I watched him go out. Frankie smiled at him as he went. Mr. Sing didn't look at him. He was a smooth-looking Chink all right. Some Chink.

Frankie came over to the table. "Well?" he said.

"Where did you know Mr. Sing?"

"He ships Chinamen," Frankie said. "Big business."

"How long you know him?"

"He's here about two years," Frankie said. "Another one ship them before him. Somebody kill him."

"Somebody will kill Mr. Sing, too."

"Sure," said Frankie. "Why not? Plenty big business."

"Some business," I said.

"Big business," said Frankie. "Ship Chinamen never come back. Other Chinamen write letters say everything fine."

"Wonderful," I said.

"This kind of Chinamen no understand write. Chinamen can write all rich. Eat nothing. Live on rice. Hundred thousand Chinamen here. Only three Chinese women."

"Why?"

"Government no let."

"Hell of a situation," I said.

"You do business him?"

"Maybe."

"Good business," said Frankie. "Better than politics. Much money. Plenty big business."

"Have a bottle of beer," I told him.

"You not worry any more?"

"Hell no," I said. "Plenty big business. Much obliged."

"Good," said Frankie and patted me on the back. "Make me happier than nothing. All I want is you happy. Chinamen good business, eh?"

"Wonderful."

"Make me happy," said Frankie. I saw he was about ready to cry because he was so pleased everything was all right, so I patted him on the back. Some Frankie.

First thing in the morning I got hold of the broker and told him to clear us. He wanted the crew list and I told him nobody.

"You're going to cross alone, Captain?"

"That's right."

"What's become of your mate?"

"He's on a drunk," I told him.

"It's very dangerous to go alone."

"It's only ninety miles," I said. "Do you think having a rummy on board makes any difference?"

I ran her over to the Standard Oil dock across the harbor and filled up both the tanks. She held nearly two hundred gallons when I had her full. I hated to buy it at twenty-eight cents a gallon but I didn't know where we might go.

Ever since I'd seen the Chink and taken the money I'd been worrying about the business. I don't think I slept all night. I brought her back to the San Francisco dock, and there was Eddy waiting on the dock for me.

"Hello, Harry," he said to me and waved. I threw him the stern line and he made her fast and then came aboard; longer, blearier, drunker than ever. I didn't say anything to him.

"What do you think about that fellow Johnson going off like that, Harry?" he asked me. "What do you know about that?"

"Get out of here," I told him. "You're poison to me."

"Brother, don't I feel as bad about it as you do?"

"Get off of her," I told him.

He just settled back in the chair and stretched his legs out. "I hear we're going across today," he said. "Well, I guess there isn't any use to stay around."

"You're not going."

"What's the matter, Harry? There's no sense to get plugged with me."

"No? Get off her."

"Oh, take it easy."

I hit him in the face and he stood up and then climbed up onto the dock.

"I wouldn't do a thing like that to you, Harry," he said.

"You're goddamn right you wouldn't," I told him. "I'm not going to carry you. That's all."

"Well, what did you have to hit me for?"

"So you'd believe it."

"What do you want me to do? Stay here and starve?"

"Starve, hell," I said. "You can get back on the ferry. You can work your way back."

"You aren't treating me square," he said.

"Who did you ever treat square, you rummy?" I told him. "You'd double-cross your own mother."

That was true, too. But I felt bad about hitting him. You know how you feel when you hit a drunk. But I wouldn't carry him the way things were now; not even if I wanted to.

He started to walk off down the dock looking longer than a day without breakfast. Then he turned and came back.

"How's to let me take a couple of dollars, Harry?"

I gave him a five-dollar bill of the Chink's.

"I always knew you were my pal. Harry, why don't you carry me?"

"You're bad luck."

"You're just plugged," he said. "Never mind, old pal. You'll be glad to see me yet."

Now he had money he went off a good deal faster but I tell you it was poison to see him walk, even. He walked just like his joints were backwards.

I went up to the Perla and met the broker and he gave me the papers and I bought him a drink. Then I had lunch and Frankie came in.

"Fellow gave me this for you," he said and handed me a rolled-up sort of tube wrapped in paper and tied with a piece of red string. It looked like a photograph when I unwrapped it and I unrolled it thinking it was maybe a picture some one around the dock had taken of the boat.

All right. It was a close-up picture of the head and chest of a dead nigger with his throat cut clear across from ear to ear and then stitched up neat and a card on his chest saying in Spanish: "This is what we do to *lenguas largas*."

"Who gave it to you?" I asked Frankie.

He pointed out a Spanish boy that works around the docks who is just about gone with the con. This kid was standing at the lunch counter.

"Ask him to come over."

The kid came over. He said two young fellows gave it to him about eleven o'clock. They asked him if he knew me and he said, Yes. Then he gave it to Frankie for me. They gave him a dollar to see that I got it. They were well dressed, he said.

"Politics," Frankie said.

"Oh, yes," I said.

"They think you told the police you were meeting those boys here that morning."

"Oh, yes."

"Bad politics," Frankie said. "Good thing you go."

"Did they leave any message?" I asked the Spanish boy.

"No," he said. "Just to give you that."

"I'm going to leave now," I said to Frankie.

"Bad politics," Frankie said. "Very bad politics."

I had all the papers in a bunch that the broker had given me and I paid the bill and walked out of that café and across the square and through the gate and I was plenty glad to come through the warehouse and get out on the dock. Those kids had me spooked all right. They were just dumb enough to think I'd tipped somebody off about that other lot. Those kids were like Pancho. When they were scared they got excited, and when they got excited they wanted to kill somebody.

I got on board and warmed up the engine. Frankie stood on the dock watching. He was smiling that funny deaf smile. I went back to him.

"Listen," I said. "Don't you get in any trouble about this."

He couldn't hear me. I had to yell it at him.

"Me good politics," Frankie said. He cast her off.

CHAPTER THREE

I WAVED to Frankie, who'd thrown the bowline on board, and I headed her out of the slip and dropped down the channel with her. A British freighter was going out and I ran along beside her and passed her. She was loaded deep with sugar and her plates were rusty. A limey in an old blue sweater looked down at me from her stern as I went by her. I went out the harbor and past the Morro and put her on the course for Key West; due north. I left the wheel and went forward and coiled up the bowline and then came back and held her on her course, spreading Havana out astern, and then dropping it off behind us as we brought the mountains up.

I dropped the Morro out of sight after a while and then the National Hotel and finally I could just see the dome of the Capitol. There wasn't much current compared to the last day we had fished and there was only a light breeze. I saw a couple of smacks headed in toward Havana and they were coming from the westward, so I knew the current was light.

I cut the switch and killed the motor. There wasn't any sense in wasting gas. I'd let her drift. When it got dark I could always pick up the light of the

Morro or, if she drifted up too far, the lights of Cojimar, and steer in and run along to Bacuranao. I figured the way the current looked she would drift the
twelve miles up to Bacuranao by dark and I'd see the
lights of Baracoa.

Well, I killed the engine and climbed up forward
to have a look around. All there was to see was the
two smacks off to the westward headed in, and way
back the dome of the Capitol standing up white out
of the edge of the sea. There was some gulfweed on
the Stream and a few birds working, but not many. I
sat up there awhile on top of the house and watched,
but the only fish I saw were those little brown ones
that use around the gulfweed. Brother, don't let anybody tell you there isn't plenty of water between Havana and Key West. I was just on the edge of it.

After a while I went down into the cockpit again,
and there was Eddy.

"What's the matter? What's the matter with the
engine?"

"She broke down."

"Why haven't you got the hatch up?"

"Oh, hell!" I said.

Do you know what he'd done? He'd come back
again and slipped the forward hatch and gone down
into the cabin and gone to sleep. He had two quarts
with him. He'd gone into the first bodega he'd seen
and bought it and come aboard. When I started out
he woke up and went back to sleep again. When I

stopped her out in the gulf and she began to roll a little with the swell it woke him up.

"I knew you'd carry me, Harry," he said.

"Carry you to hell," I said. "You aren't even on the
crew list. I've got a good mind to make you jump
overboard now."

"You're an old joker, Harry," he said. "Us Conchs
ought to stick together when we're in trouble."

"You," I said, "with your mouth. Who's going to
trust your mouth when you're hot?"

"I'm a good man, Harry. You put me to the test
and see what a good man I am."

"Get me the two quarts," I told him. I was thinking of something else.

He brought them out and I took a drink from the
open one and put them forward by the wheel. He
stood there and I looked at him. I was sorry for him
and for what I knew I'd have to do. Hell, I knew him
when he was a good man.

"What's the matter with her, Harry?"

"She's all right."

"What's the matter, then? What are you looking at
me like that for?"

"Brother," I told him, and I was sorry for him,
"you're in plenty of trouble."

"What do you mean, Harry?"

"I don't know yet," I said. "I haven't got it all figured out yet."

We sat there awhile and I didn't feel like talking

to him any more. Once I knew it, it was hard to talk to him. Then I went below and got out the pump-gun and the Winchester .30–30 that I always had below in the cabin and hung them up in their cases from the top of the house where we hung the rods usually, right over the wheel where I could reach them. I keep them in those full-length, clipped sheep's wool cases with the wool inside soaked in oil. That's the only way you can keep them from rusting on a boat.

I loosened up the pump and worked her a few times, and then filled her up and pumped one into the barrel. I put a shell in the chamber of the Winchester and filled up the magazine. I got out the Smith and Wesson thirty-eight special I had when I was on the police force up in Miami from under the mattress and cleaned and oiled it and filled it up and put it on my belt.

"What's the matter?" Eddy said. "What the hell's the matter?"

"Nothing," I told him.

"What's all the damn guns for?"

"I always carry them on board," I said. "To shoot birds that bother the baits or to shoot sharks, or for cruising along the keys."

"What's the matter, damn it?" said Eddy. "What's the matter?"

"Nothing," I told him. I sat there with the old thirty-eight flopping against my leg when she rolled, and I looked at him. I thought, there's no sense to do it now. I'm going to need him now.

"We're going to do a little job," I said. "In at Bacuranao. I'll tell you what to do when it's time."

I didn't want to tell him too far ahead because he would get to worrying and get so spooked he wouldn't be any use.

"You couldn't have anybody better than me, Harry," he said. "I'm the man for you. I'm with you on anything."

I looked at him, tall and bleary and shaky, and I didn't say anything.

"Listen, Harry. Would you give me just one?" he asked me. "I don't want to get the shakes."

I gave him one and we sat and waited for it to get dark. It was a fine sunset and there was a nice light breeze, and when the sun got pretty well down I started the engine and headed her in slow toward land.

CHAPTER FOUR

WE LAY offshore about a mile in the dark. The current had freshened up, with the sun down, and I noticed it running in. I could see the Morro light way down to the westward and the glow of Havana, and the lights opposite us were Rincōn and Baracoa. I headed her up against the current until I was past Bacuranao and nearly to Cojimar. Then I let her drift down. It was plenty dark but I could tell good where we were. I had all the lights out.

"What's it going to be, Harry?" Eddy asked me. He was beginning to be spooked again.

"What do you think?"

"I don't know," he said. "You've got me worried." He was pretty close to the shakes and when he came near me he had a breath like a buzzard.

"What time is it?"

"I'll go down and see," he said. He came back up and said it was half past nine.

"Are you hungry?" I asked him.

"No," he said. "You know I couldn't eat, Harry."

"All right," I told him. "You can have one."

After he had it I asked him how he felt. He said he felt fine.

"I'm going to give you a couple more in a little while," I told him. "I know you haven't got any *co-jones* unless you've got rum and there isn't much on board. So you'd better go easy."

"Tell me what's up," said Eddy.

"Listen," I said, talking to him in the dark. "We're going to Bacuranao and pick up twelve Chinks. You take the wheel when I tell you to and do what I tell you to. We'll take the twelve Chinks on board and we'll lock them below forward. Go on forward now and fasten the hatch from the outside."

He went up and I saw him shadowed against the dark. He came back and he said, "Harry, can I have one of those now?"

"No," I said. "I want you rum-brave. I don't want you useless."

"I'm a good man, Harry. You'll see."

"You're a rummy," I said. "Listen. One Chink is going to bring those twelve out. He's going to give me some money at the start. When they're all on board he's going to give me some more money. When you see him start to hand me money the second time you put her ahead and hook her up and head her out to sea. Don't you pay any attention to what happens. You keep her going out no matter what happens. Do you understand?"

"Yes."

"If any Chink starts bursting out of the cabin or coming through the hatch, once we're out and under way, you take that pump-gun and blow them back as fast as they come out. Do you know how to use the pump-gun?"

"No. But you can show me."

"You'd never remember. Do you know how to use the Winchester?"

"Just pump the lever and shoot it."

"That's right," I said. "Only don't shoot any holes in the hull."

"You'd better give me that other drink," Eddy said.

"All right. I'll give you a little one."

I gave him a real one. I knew they wouldn't make him drunk now; not pouring them into all that fear. But each one would work for a little while. After he drank this Eddy said, just as though he was happy, "So we're going to run Chinks. Well, by God, I always said I'd run Chinamen if I was ever broke."

"But you never got broke before, eh?" I said to him. He was funny all right.

I gave him three more drinks to keep him brave before it was half past ten. It was funny watching him and it kept me from thinking about it myself. I hadn't figured on all this wait. I'd planned to leave after dark, run out, just out of the glare, and coast along to Cojimar.

At a little before eleven I saw the two lights show on the point. I waited a little while and then I took her in slow. Bacuranao is a cove where there used to be a big dock for loading sand. There is a little river that comes in when the rains open the bar across the mouth. The northers, in the winter, pile the sand up and close it. They used to go in with schooners and load guavas from the river and there used to be a town. But the hurricane took it and it is all gone now except one house that some Gallegos built out of the shacks the hurricane blew down and that they use for a clubhouse on Sundays when they come out to swim and picnic from Havana. There is one other house where the delegate lives but it is back from the beach.

Each little place like that all down the coast has a government delegate, but I figured the Chink must use his own boat and have him fixed. As we came in I could smell the sea grape and that sweet smell from the brush you get off the land.

"Get up forward," I said to Eddy.

"You can't hit anything on that side," he said. "The reef's on the other side as you go in." You see, he'd been a good man once.

"Watch her," I said, and I took her in to where I know they could see us. With no surf they could hear the engine. I didn't want to wait around, not knowing whether they saw us or not, so I flashed the running lights on once, just the green and red, and turned them off. Then I turned her and headed her out and let her lay there, just outside, with the engine just ticking. There was quite a little swell that close in.

"Come on back here," I said to Eddy and I gave him a real drink.

"Do you cock it first with your thumb?" he whispered to me. He was sitting at the wheel now, and I had reached up and had both the cases open and the butts pulled out about six inches.

"That's right."

"Oh, boy," he said.

It certainly was wonderful what a drink would do to him and how quick.

We lay there and I could see a light from the delegate's house back through the brush. I saw the two lights on the point go down, and one of them moving off around the point. They must have blown the other one out.

Then, in a little while, coming out of the cove, I see a boat come toward us with a man sculling. I could tell by the way he swung back and forth. I knew he had a big oar. I was pretty pleased. If they were sculling that meant one man.

They came alongside.

"Good evening, captain," said Mr. Sing.

"Come astern and put her broadside," I said to him.

He said something to the kid who was sculling but he couldn't scull her backwards, so I took hold of the gunwale and passed her astern. There were eight men in the boat. The six Chinks, Mr. Sing, and the kid sculling. While I was pulling her astern I was waiting for something to hit me on top of the head but nothing did. I straightened up and let Mr. Sing hold onto the stern.

"Let's see what it looks like," I said.

He handed it to me and I took the roll of it up to where Eddy was at the wheel and put on the binnacle light. I looked at it carefully. It looked all right to me and I turned off the light. Eddy was trembling.

"Pour yourself one," I said. I saw him reach for the bottle and tip it up.

I went back to the stern.

"All right," I said. "Let six come on board."

Mr. Sing and the Cuban that sculled were having a job holding their boat from knocking in what little swell there was. I heard Mr. Sing say something in Chink and all the Chinks in the boat started to climb onto the stern.

"One at a time," I said.

He said something again, and then one after another six Chinks came over the stern. They were all lengths and sizes.

"Show them forward," I said to Eddy.

"Right this way, gentlemen," said Eddy. By God, I knew he had taken a big one.

"Lock the cabin," I said, when they were all in.

"Yes, sir," said Eddy.

"I will return with the others," said Mr. Sing.

"O.K.," I told him.

I pushed them clear and the boy with him started sculling off.

"Listen," I said to Eddy. "You lay off that bottle. You're brave enough now."

"O.K., chief," said Eddy.

"What's the matter with you?"

"This is what I like to do," said Eddy. "You say you just pull it backward with your thumb?"

"You lousy rummy," I told him. "Give me a drink out of that."

"All gone," said Eddy. "Sorry, chief."

"Listen. What you have to do now is watch when he hands me the money and put her ahead."

"O.K., chief," said Eddy.

I reached up and took the other bottle and got the corkscrew and drew the cork. I took a good drink and went back to the stern, putting the cork in tight and laying the bottle behind two wicker jugs full of water.

"Here comes Mr. Sing," I said to Eddy.

"Yes, sir," said Eddy.

The boat came out sculling toward us.

He brought her astern and I let them do the holding on. Mr. Sing had hold of the roller we had across the stern to slide a big fish aboard.

"Let them come aboard," I said, "one at a time."

Six more assorted Chinks came on board over the stern.

"Open up and show them forward," I told Eddy.

"Yes, sir," said Eddy.

"Lock the cabin."

"Yes, sir."

I saw he was at the wheel.

"All right, Mr. Sing," I said. "Let's see the rest of it."

He put his hand in his pocket and reached the money out toward me. I reached for it and grabbed his wrist with the money in his hand, and as he came forward on the stern I grabbed his throat with the other hand. I felt her start and then churn ahead as she hooked up and I was plenty busy with Mr. Sing but I could see the Cuban standing in the stern of the boat holding the sculling oar as we pulled away from her through all the flopping and bouncing Mr. Sing was doing. He was flopping and bouncing worse than any dolphin on a gaff.

I got his arm around behind him and came up on it but I brought it too far because I felt it go. When it went he made a funny little noise and came forward, me holding him throat and all, and bit me in the shoulder. But when I felt the arm go I dropped it. It wasn't any good to him any more and I took him by the throat with both hands, and brother, that Mr. Sing would flop just like a fish, true, his loose arm flailing. But I got him forward onto his knees and had both thumbs well in behind his talk-box, and I bent the whole thing back until she cracked. Don't think you can't hear it crack, either.

I held him quiet just a second, and then I laid him down across the stern. He lay there, face up, quiet, in his good clothes, with his feet in the cockpit; and I left him.

I picked up the money off the cockpit floor and took it up and put on the binnacle light and counted it. Then I took the wheel and told Eddy to look under the stern for some pieces of iron that I used for anchoring whenever we fished bottom-fishing on patches or rocky bottom where you wouldn't want to risk an anchor.

"I can't find anything," he said. He was scared being down there by Mr. Sing.

"Take the wheel," I said. "Keep her out."

There was a certain amount of moving around going on below but I wasn't spooked about them.

I found a couple of pieces of what I wanted, iron from the old coaling dock at Tortugas, and I took some snapper line and made a couple of good big pieces fast to Mr. Sing's ankles. Then when we were about two miles offshore I slid him over. He slid over smooth off the roller. I never even looked in his pockets. I didn't feel like fooling with him.

He'd bled a little on the stern from his nose and his mouth, and I dipped a bucket of water that nearly pulled me overboard the way we were going, and cleaned her off good with a scrub brush from under the stern.

"Slow her down," I said to Eddy.

"What if he floats up?" Eddy said.

"I dropped him in about seven hundred fathoms," I said. "He's going down all that way. That's a long way, brother. He won't float till the gas brings him up and all the time he's going with the current and baiting up fish. Hell," I said, "you don't have to worry about Mr. Sing."

"What did you have against him?" Eddy asked me.

"Nothing," I said. "He was the easiest man to do business with I ever met. I thought there must be something wrong all the time."

"What did you kill him for?"

"To keep from killing twelve other Chinks," I told him.

"Harry," he said, "you've got to give me one because I can feel them coming on. It made me sick to see his head all loose like that."

So I gave him one.

"What about the Chinks?" Eddy said.

"I want to get them out as quick as I can," I told him. "Before they smell up the cabin."

"Where are you going to put them?"

"We'll run them right in to the long beach," I told him.

"Take her in now?"

"Sure," I said. "Take her in slow."

We came in slow over the reef and to where I could see the beach shine. There is plenty of water over the reef and inside it's all sandy bottom and slopes right into shore.

"Get up forward and give me the depth."

He kept sounding with a grains pole, motioning me on with the pole. He came back and motioned me to stop. I came astern on her.

"You've got about five feet."

"We've got to anchor," I said. "If anything happens so we haven't time to get her up, we can cut loose or break her off."

Eddy paid out rope and when finally she didn't drag he made her fast. She swung stern in.

"It's sandy bottom, you know," he said.

"How much water have we got at the stern?"

"Not over five feet."

"You take the rifle," I said. "And be careful."

"Let me have one," he said. He was plenty nervous.

I gave him one and took down the pump-gun. I unlocked the cabin door, opened it, and said: "Come on out."

Nothing happened.

Then one Chink put his head out and saw Eddy standing there with a rifle and ducked back.

"Come on out. Nobody's going to hurt you," I said.

Nothing doing. Only lots of talk in Chink.

"Come on out, you!" Eddy said. My God, I knew he'd had the bottle.

"Put that bottle away," I said to him, "or I'll blow you out of the boat."

"Come on out," I said to them, "or I'll shoot in at you."

I saw one of them looking at the corner of the door and he saw the beach evidently because he begins to chatter.

"Come on," I said, "or I'll shoot."

Out they came.

Now I tell you it would take a hell of a mean man to butcher a bunch of Chinks like that and I'll bet there would be plenty of trouble, too, let alone mess.

They came out and they were scared and they didn't have any guns but there were twelve of them. I walked backwards down to the stern holding the pump-gun. "Get overboard," I said. "It's not over your heads."

Nobody moved.

"Over you go."

Nobody moved.

"You yellow rat-eating aliens," Eddy said, "get overboard."

"Shut your drunken mouth," I told him.

"No swim," one Chink said.

"No need swim," I said. "No deep."

"Come on, get overboard," Eddy said.

"Come astern here," I said. "Take your gun in one hand and your grain pole in the other and show them how deep it is."

He showed them, holding up the wet pole.

"No need swim?" the one asked me.

"No."

"True?"

"Yes."

"Where we?"

"Cuba."

"You damn crook," he said and went over the side, hanging on and then letting go. His head went under but he came up and his chin was out of water. "Damn crook," he said. "Goddamn crook."

He was mad and plenty brave. He said something in Chink and the others started going into the water off the stern.

"All right," I said to Eddy. "Get the anchor up."

As we headed her out, the moon started to come up, and you could see the Chinks with just their heads out of water, walking ashore, and the shine of the beach and the brush behind.

We got out past the reef and I looked back once and saw the beach and the mountains starting to show up; then I put her on her course for Key West.

"Now you can take a sleep," I said to Eddy. "No, wait, go below and open all the ports to get the stink out and bring me the iodine."

"What's the matter?" he said when he brought it.

"I cut my finger."

"Do you want me to steer?"

"Get a sleep," I said. "I'll wake you up."

He lay down on the built-in bunk in the cockpit, over the gas tank, and in a little while he was asleep.

CHAPTER FIVE

I HELD the wheel with my knee and opened up my shirt and saw where Mr. Sing bit me. It was quite a bite and I put iodine on it, and then I sat there steering and wondering whether a bite from a Chinaman was poisonous, and listened to her running nice and smooth and the water washing along her and I figured, Hell, no, that bite wasn't poisonous. A man like that Mr. Sing probably scrubbed his teeth two or three times a day. Some Mr. Sing. He certainly wasn't much of a business man. Maybe he was. Maybe he just trusted me. I tell you I couldn't figure him.

Well, now it was all simple except for Eddy. Because he's a rummy he'll talk when he gets hot. I sat there steering and I looked at him and I thought, hell, he's as well off dead as the way he is, and then I'm all clear. When I found he was on board I decided I'd have to do away with him but then when everything had come out so nice I didn't have the heart. But looking at him lying there it certainly was a temptation. But then I thought there's no sense spoiling it by doing something you'd be sorry for afterwards. Then I started to think he wasn't even on the crew list and I'd have to pay a fine for bringing him in and I didn't know how to consider him.

Well, I had plenty of time to think about it and I held her on her course and every once in a while I'd take a drink out of the bottle he'd brought on board. There wasn't much in it, and when I'd finished it, I opened up the only one I had left, and I tell you I felt pretty good steering, and it was a pretty night to cross. It had turned out a good trip all right, finally, even though it had looked plenty bad plenty of times.

When it got daylight Eddy woke up. He said he felt terrible.

"Take the wheel a minute," I told him. "I want to look around."

I went back to the stern and threw a little water on her. But she was perfectly clean. I scrubbed the brush over the side. I unloaded the guns and stowed them below. But I still kept the gun on my belt. It was fresh and nice as you want it below, no smell at all. A little water had come in through the starboard port onto one of the bunks was all; so I shut the ports. There wasn't a customhouse officer in the world could smell Chink in her now.

I saw the clearance papers in the net bag hanging up under her framed license where I'd shoved them when I came on board and I took them out to look them over. Then I went up to the cockpit.

"Listen," I said. "How did you get on the crew list?"

"I met the broker when he was leaving for the consulate and told him I was going."

"God looks after rummies," I told him and I took the thirty-eight off and stowed it down below.

I made some coffee down below and then I came up and took the wheel.

"There's coffee below," I told him.

"Brother, coffee wouldn't do me any good." You know you had to be sorry for him. He certainly looked bad.

About nine o'clock we saw the Sand Key light just about dead ahead. We'd seen tankers going up the Gulf for quite a while.

"We'll be in in a couple of hours now," I said to him. "I'm going to give you the same four dollars a day just as if Johnson had paid."

"How much did you get out of last night?" he asked me.

"Only six hundred," I told him.

I don't know whether he believed me or not.

"Don't I share in it?"

"That's your share," I told him. "What I just told you, and if you ever open your mouth about last night I'll hear of it and I'll do away with you."

"You know I'm no squealer, Harry."

"You're a rummy. But no matter how rum dumb you get, if you ever talk about that, I promise you."

"I'm a good man," he said. "You oughtn't to talk to me like that."

"They can't make it fast enough to keep you a good man," I told him. But I didn't worry about him any more because who was going to believe him? Mr. Sing wouldn't make any complaints. The Chinks weren't going to. You know the boy that sculled them out wasn't. He wouldn't want to get himself in trouble. Eddy would mouth about it sooner or later, maybe, but who believes a rummy?

Why, who could prove anything? Naturally it would have made plenty more talk when they saw his name on the crew list. That was luck for me, all right. I could have said he fell overboard, but it makes plenty talk. Plenty of luck for Eddy, too. Plenty of luck, all right.

Then we came to the edge of the stream and the water quit being blue and was light and greenish and inside I could see the stakes on the Eastern and the Western Dry Rocks and the wireless masts at Key West and the La Concha hotel up high out of all the low houses and plenty smoke from out where they're burning garbage. Sand Key light was plenty close now and you could see the boathouse and the little dock alongside the light and I knew we were only forty minutes away now and I felt good to be getting back and I had a good stake now for the summertime.

"What do you say about a drink, Eddy?" I said to him.

"Ah, Harry," he said, "I always knew you were my pal."

That night I was sitting in the living room smoking a cigar and drinking a whiskey and water and listening to Gracie Allen on the radio. The girls had gone to the show and sitting there I felt sleepy and I felt good. There was somebody at the front door and Marie, my wife, got up from where she was sitting and went to it. She came back and said, "It's that rummy, Eddy Marshall. He says he's got to see you."

"Tell him to get out before I run him out," I told her.

She came back in and sat down and looking out the window where I was sitting with my feet up I could see Eddy going along the road under the arc light with another rummy he'd picked up, the two of them swaying, and their shadows from the arc light swaying worse.

"Poor goddamned rummies," Marie said. "I pity a rummy."

"He's a lucky rummy."

"There ain't any lucky rummies," Marie said. "You know that, Harry."

"No," I said. "I guess there aren't."

PART TWO
HARRY MORGAN
(Fall)

CHAPTER SIX

THEY CAME on across in the night and it blew a big breeze from the northwest. When the sun was up he sighted a tanker coming down the Gulf and she stood up so high and white with the sun on her in that cold air it looked like tall buildings rising out of the sea and he said to the nigger, "Where the hell are we?"

The nigger raised himself up to look.

"Ain't nothing like that this side of Miami."

"You know damn well we ain't been carried up to no Miami," he told the nigger.

"All I say ain't no buildings like that on no Florida Keys."

"We've been steering for Sand Key."

"We got to see it then. It or American shoals."

Then in a little while he saw it was a tanker and not buildings and then in less than an hour he saw Sand Key light, straight, thin and brown rising out of the sea right where it ought to be.

"You got to have confidence steering," he told the nigger.

"I got confidence," the nigger said. "But the way this trip gone I ain't got confidence no more."

"How's your leg?"

"It hurts me all the time."

"It ain't nothing," the man said. "You keep it clean and wrapped up and it'll heal by its-self."

He was steering to the westward now to go in to lay up for the day in the mangroves by Woman Key where he would not see anybody and where the boat was to come out to meet them.

"You're going to be all right," he told the nigger.

"I don't know," the nigger said. "I hurt bad."

"I'm going to fix you up good when we get in to the place," he told him. "You aren't shot bad. Quit worrying."

"I'm shot," he said. "I ain't never been shot before. Any way I'm shot is bad."

"You're just scared."

"No, sir. I'm shot. And I'm hurting bad. I've been throbbing all night."

The nigger went on grumbling like that and he could not keep from taking the bandage off to look at it.

"Leave it alone," the man who was steering told him. The nigger lay on the floor of the cockpit and there were sacks of liquor, shaped like hams, piled everywhere. He had made himself a place in them to lay down in. Every time he moved there was the noise of broken glass in the sacks and there was the odor of spilled liquor. The liquor had run all over everything. The man was steering in for Woman Key now. He could see it now plainly.

"I hurt," the nigger said. "I hurt worse all the time."

"I'm sorry, Wesley," the man said. "But I got to steer."

"You treat a man no better than a dog," the nigger said. He was getting ugly now. But the man was still sorry for him.

"I'm going to make you comfortable, Wesley," he said. "You lay quiet now."

"You don't care what happens to a man," the nigger said. "You ain't hardly human."

"I'm going to fix you up good," the man said. "You just lay quiet."

"You ain't going to fix me up," the nigger said. The man, whose name was Harry Morgan, said nothing then because he liked the nigger and there was nothing to do now but hit him, and he couldn't hit him. The nigger kept on talking.

"Why didn't we stop when they started shooting?"

The man did not answer.

"Ain't a man's life worth more than a load of liquor?"

The man was intent on his steering.

"All we have to do is stop and let them take the liquor."

"No," the man said. "They take the liquor and the boat and you go to jail."

"I don't mind jail," the nigger said. "But I never wanted to get shot."

He was getting on the man's nerves now and the man was becoming tired of hearing him talk.

"Who the hell's shot worse?" he asked him. "You or me?"

"You're shot worse," the nigger said. "But I ain't never been shot. I didn't figure to get shot. I ain't paid to get shot. I don't want to be shot."

"Take it easy, Wesley," the man told him. "It don't do you any good to talk like that."

They were coming up on the Key now. They were inside the shoals and as he headed her into the channel it was hard to see with the sun on the water. The nigger was going out of his head, or becoming religious because he was hurt; anyway he was talking all the time.

"Why they run liquor now?" he said. "Prohibition's over. Why they keep up a traffic like that? Whyn't they bring the liquor in on the ferry?"

The man steering was watching the channel closely.

"Why don't people be honest and decent and make a decent honest living?"

The man saw where the water was rippling smooth off the bank even when he could not see the bank in the sun and he turned her off. He swung her around, spinning the wheel with one arm, and then the channel opened out and he took her slowly right up to the edge of the mangroves. He came astern on the engines and threw out the two clutches.

"I can put an anchor down," he said. "But I can't get no anchor up."

"I can't even move," the nigger said.

"You're certainly in a hell of a shape," the man told him.

He had a difficult time breaking out, lifting, and dropping the small anchor but he got it over and paid out quite a lot of rope and the boat swung in against the mangroves so they came right into the cockpit. Then he went back and down into the cockpit. He thought the cockpit was a hell of a sight, all right.

All night after he had dressed the nigger's wound and the nigger had bandaged his arm he had been watching the compass, steering, and when it came daylight he had seen the nigger laying there in the sacks in the middle of the cockpit, but then he was watching the seas and the compass and looking for the Sand Key light and he had never observed carefully how things were. Things were bad.

The nigger was lying in the middle of the load of sacked liquor with his leg up. There were eight bullet holes through the cockpit splintered wide. The glass was broken in the windshield. He did not know how much stuff was smashed and wherever the nigger had not bled, he, himself, had bled. But the worst thing, the way he felt at the moment, was the smell of booze. Everything was soaked in it. Now the boat was lying quietly against the mangroves but he could not stop feeling the motion of the big sea they had been in all night in the Gulf.

"I'm going to make some coffee," he told the nigger. "Then I'll fix you up again."

"I don't want no coffee."

"I do," the man told him. But down below he began to feel dizzy so he came out on deck again.

"I guess we won't have coffee," he said.

"I want some water."

"All right."

He gave the negro a cup of water out of a demijohn.

"Why you want to keep on running for when they started to shoot?"

"Why they want to shoot?" the man answered.

"I want a doctor," the nigger told him.

"What's a doctor going to do that I ain't done for you?"

"Doctor going to cure me."

"You'll have a doctor tonight when the boat comes out."

"I don't want to wait for no boat."

"All right," the man said. "We're going to dump this liquor now."

He started to dump it and it was hard work one handed. A sack of liquor only weighs forty pounds but he had not dumped very many of them before he became dizzy again. He sat down in the cockpit and then he lay down.

"You going to kill youself," the nigger said.

The man lay quietly in the cockpit with his head

against one of the sacks. The branches of the mangroves had come into the cockpit and they made
a shadow over him where he lay. He could hear
the wind above the mangroves and looking out at the
high, cold sky, see the thin-blown clouds of the
norther.

"Nobody going to come out with this breeze," he
thought. "They won't look for us to have started with
this blowing."

"You think they'll come out?" the nigger asked.

"Sure," the man said. "Why not?"

"It's blowing too hard."

"They're looking for us."

"Not with it like this. What you want to lie to me
for?" The nigger was talking with his mouth almost
against a sack.

"Take it easy, Wesley," the man told him.

"Take it easy, the man says," the nigger went on.
"Take it easy. Take what easy? Take dyin' like a dog
easy? You got me here. Get me out."

"Take it easy," the man said, kindly.

"They ain't coming," the nigger said. "I know they
ain't coming. I'm cold, I tell you. I can't stand this
pain and cold, I tell you."

The man sat up feeling hollow and unsteady. The
nigger's eyes watched him as he rose on one knee,
his right arm dangling, took the hand of his right
arm in his left hand and placed it between his knees
and then pulled himself up by the plank nailed above

the gunwale until he stood, looking down, down at the nigger, his right hand still held between his thighs. He was thinking that he had never really felt pain before.

"If I keep it out straight, pulled out straight, it don't hurt so bad," he said.

"Let me tie it up in a sling," the nigger said.

"I can't make a bend in the elbow," the man said. "It stiffened that way."

"What we going to do?"

"Dump this liquor," the man told him. "Can't you put over what you can reach, Wesley?"

The nigger tried to move to reach a sack, then groaned and lay back.

"Do you hurt that bad, Wesley?"

"Oh, God," the nigger said.

"You don't think once you moved it, it wouldn't hurt so bad?"

"I'm shot," the nigger said. "I ain't going to move. The man wants me to go to dumpin' liquor when I'm shot."

"Take it easy."

"You say that once more I go crazy."

"Take it easy," the man said quietly.

The nigger made a howling noise and, shuffling with his hands on the deck, picked up the whetstone from under the coaming.

"I'll kill you," he said. "I'll cut your heart out."

"Not with no whetstone," the man said. "Take it easy, Wesley."

The nigger blubbered with his face against a sack. The man went on slowly lifting the sacked packages of liquor and dropping them over the side.

CHAPTER SEVEN

WHILE HE was dumping the liquor he heard the sound of a motor and looking saw a boat headed toward them, coming down the channel around the end of the key. It was a white boat with a buff painted house and a windshield.

"Boat coming," he said. "Come on, Wesley."

"I can't."

"I'm remembering from now on," the man said. "Before was different."

"Go ahead and remember," the nigger told him. "I ain't forgot nothing either."

Working fast now, the sweat running down his face, not stopping to watch the boat coming slowly down the channel, the man picked up the sacked packages of liquor with his good arm and dropped them over the side.

"Roll over," he reached for the package under the nigger's head and swung it over the side. The nigger sat up.

"Here they are," he said. The boat was almost abeam of them.

"It's Captain Willie," the nigger said. "With a party."

In the stern of the white boat two men in flannels and white cloth hats sat in fishing chairs trolling and an old man in a felt hat and a windbreaker held the tiller and steered the boat close past the mangroves where the booze boat lay.

"What do you say, Harry?" the old man called as he passed. The man called Harry waved his good arm in reply. The boat went on past, the two men who were fishing looking towards the booze boat and talking to the old man. Harry could not hear what they were saying.

"He'll make a turn at the mouth and come back," Harry said to the negro. He went below and came up with a blanket. "Let me cover you up."

"'Bout time you cover me up. They couldn't help but see that liquor. What we goin' to do?"

"Willie's a good skate," the man said. "He'll tell them in town we're out here. Those fellows fishing ain't going to bother us. What they care about us?"

He felt very shaky now and he sat down on the steering seat and held his right arm tight between his thighs. His knees were shaking and with the shaking he could feel the ends of the bone in his upper arm grate. He opened his knees, lifted his arm out, and let it hang by his side. He was sitting there, his arm hanging, when the boat passed them coming back up the channel. The two men in the fishing chairs were talking. They had put up their rods and one of them was looking at him through a pair of glasses. They

were too far out for him to hear what they were saying. It would not have helped him if he had.

On board the charter boat *South Florida,* trolling
down the Woman Key channel, because it was too
rough to go out to the reef, Captain Willie Adams
was thinking, so Harry crossed last night. That boy's
got *cojones.* He must have got that whole blow. She's
a sea boat all right. How you suppose he smashed his
windshield? Damned if I'd cross a night like last
night. Damned if I'd ever run liquor from Cuba.
They bring it all from Mariel now. It's supposed to be
wide open. "What's that you say, Cap?"

"What boat is that?" asked one of the men in the
fishing chairs.

"That boat?"

"Yes, that boat."

"Oh, that's a Key West boat."

"What I said was, whose boat is it?"

"I wouldn't know that, Cap."

"Is the owner a fisherman?"

"Well, some say he is."

"What do you mean?"

"He does a little of everything."

"You don't know his name?"

"No, sir."

"You called him Harry."

"Not me."

"I heard you call him Harry."

Captain Willie Adams took a good look at the man

who was speaking to him. He saw a high-cheekboned, thin-lipped, very ruddy face with deep set gray eyes and a contemptuous mouth looking at him from under a white canvas hat.

"I must have called him that by mistake," Captain Willie said.

"You can see that the man is wounded, Doctor," the other man said, handing the glasses to his companion.

"I can see that without glasses," the man addressed as Doctor said. "Who is that man?"

"I wouldn't know," said Captain Willie.

"Well, you will know," the man with the contemptuous mouth said. "Write down the numbers on the bow."

"I have them, Doctor."

"We'll go over and have a look," the Doctor said.

"Are you a doctor?" Captain Willie asked.

"Not of medicine," the gray-eyed man told him.

"If you're not a medical doctor I wouldn't go over there."

"Why not?"

"If he wanted us he would have signalled us. If he don't want us it's none of our business. Down here everybody aims to mind their own business."

"All right. Suppose you mind yours then. Take us over to that boat."

Captain Willie continued on his way up the channel, the two-cylinder Palmer coughing steadily.

"Didn't you hear me?"

"Yes, sir."

"Why don't you obey my order?"

"Who the hell you think you are?" asked Captain Willie.

"That's not the question. Do as I tell you."

"Who do you think you are?"

"All right. For your information, I'm one of the three most important men in the United States today."

"What the hell you doing in Key West, then?"

The other man leaned forward. "He's Frederick Harrison," he said impressively.

"I never heard of him," said Captain Willie.

"Well, you will," said Frederick Harrison. "And so will every one in this stinking jerkwater little town if I have to grub it out by the roots."

"You're a nice fellow," said Captain Willie. "How did you get so important?"

"He's one of the biggest men in the administration," said the other man.

"Nuts," said Captain Willie. "If he's all that what's he doing in Key West?"

"He's just here for a rest," the secretary explained. "He's going to be governor-general of—"

"That's enough, Willis," Frederick Harrison said. "Now will you take us over to that boat," he said smiling. He had a smile which was reserved for such occasions.

"No, sir."

"Listen, you half-witted fisherman. I'll make life so miserable for you——"

"Yes," said Captain Willie.

"You don't know who I am."

"None of it don't mean anything to me," said Captain Willie.

"That man is a bootlegger, isn't he?"

"What do *you* think?"

"There's probably a reward for him."

"I doubt that."

"He's a lawbreaker."

"He's got a family and he's got to eat and feed them. Who the hell do you eat off of with people working here in Key West for the government for six dollars and a half a week?"

"He's wounded. That means he's been in trouble."

"Unless he shot hisself for fun."

"You can save that sarcasm. You're going over to that boat and we're going to take that man and that boat into custody."

"Into where?"

"Into Key West."

"Are you an officer?"

"I've told you who he is," the secretary said.

"All right," said Captain Willie. He pushed the tiller hard over and turned the boat, coming so close to the edge of the channel that the propeller threw up a circling cloud of marl. He chugged down the channel toward where the other boat lay against the mangroves.

"Have you a gun aboard?" Frederick Harrison asked Captain Willie.

"No, sir."

The two men in flannels were standing up now watching the booze boat.

"This is better fun than fishing, eh, Doctor?" the secretary said.

"Fishing is nonsense," said Frederick Harrison. "If you catch a sailfish what do you do with it? You can't eat it. This is really interesting. I'm glad to see this at first hand. Wounded as he is that man cannot escape. It's too rough at sea. We know his boat."

"You're really capturing him single-handed," said the secretary admiringly.

"And unarmed, too," said Frederick Harrison.

"With no G men nonsense," said the secretary.

"Edgar Hoover exaggerates his publicity," said Frederick Harrison. "I feel we've given him about enough rope. Pull alongside," he said to Captain Willie. Captain Willie threw out his clutch and the boat drifted.

"Hey," Captain Willie called to the other boat. "Keep your heads down."

"What's that?" Harrison said angrily.

"Shut up," said Captain Willie. "Hey," he called over to the other boat. "Listen. Get on into town and take it easy. Never mind the boat. They'll take the

boat. Dump your load and get into town. I got a guy
here on board some kind of a stool from Washington.
More important than the president, he says. He
wants to pinch you. He thinks you're a bootlegger.
He's got the numbers of the boat. I ain't never seen
you so I don't know who you are. I couldn't identify
you—"

The boats had drifted apart. Captain Willie went
on shouting, "I don't know where this place is where
I seen you. I wouldn't know how to get back here."

"O.K.," came a shout from the booze boat.

"I'm taking this big alphabet man fishing until
dark," Captain Willie shouted.

"O.K."

"He loves to fish," Captain Willie yelled, his voice
almost breaking. "But the son of a bitch claims you
can't eat 'em."

"Thanks, brother," came the voice of Harry.

"That chap your brother?" asked Frederick Harrison, his face very red but his love for information
still unappeased.

"No, sir," said Captain Willie. "Most everybody
goes in boats calls each other brother."

"We'll go into Key West," Frederick Harrison
said; but he said it without great conviction.

"No, sir," said Captain Willie. "You gentlemen
chartered me for a day. I'm going to see you get your
money's worth. You called me a halfwit but I'll see
you get a full day's charter."

"Take us to Key West," Harrison said.

"Yes, sir," said Captain Willie. "Later on. But listen, sailfish is just as good eating as kingfish. When we used to sell them to Rios for the Havana market we got ten cents a pound same as kings."

"Oh, *shut* up," said Frederick Harrison.

"I thought you'd be interested in these things as a government man. Ain't you mixed up in the prices of things that we eat or something? Ain't that it? Making them more costly or something. Making the grits cost more and the grunts less?"

"Oh, shut up," said Harrison.

CHAPTER EIGHT

ON THE BOOZE boat Harry had the last sack over.
"Get me the fish knife," he said to the nigger.

"It's gone."

Harry pressed the self starters and started the two
engines. He'd put a second engine in her when he
went back to running liquor when the depression had
put charter boat fishing on the bum. He got the
hatchet and with his left hand chopped the anchor
rope through against the bitt. It'll sink and they'll
grapple it when they pick up the load, he thought.
I'll run her up into the Garrison Bight and if they're
going to take her they'll take her. I got to get to a
doctor. I don't want to lose my arm and the boat both.
The load is worth as much as the boat. There wasn't
much of it smashed. A little smashed can smell plenty.

He shoved the port clutch in and swung out away
from the mangroves with the tide. The engines ran
smoothly. Captain Willie's boat was two miles away
now headed for Boca Grande. I guess the tide's high
enough to go through the lakes now, Harry thought.

He shoved in his starboard clutch and the engines
roared as he pushed up the throttle. He could feel
her bow rise and the green mangroves coasted swiftly
alongside as the boat sucked the water away from

their roots. I hope they don't take her, he thought. I hope they can fix my arm. How was I to know they'd shoot at us in Mariel after we could go and come there open for six months. That's Cubans for you. Somebody didn't pay somebody so we got the shooting. That's Cubans all right.

"Hey, Wesley," he said, looking back into the cockpit where the nigger lay with the blanket over him. "How you feeling?"

"God," said Wesley. "I couldn't feel no worse."

"You'll feel worse when the old doctor probes for it," Harry told him.

"You ain't human," the nigger said. "You ain't got human feelings."

That old Willie is a good skate, Harry was thinking. There's a good skate that old Willie. We did better to come in than to wait. It was foolish to wait. I felt so dizzy and sicklike I lost my judgment.

Ahead now he could see the white of the La Concha hotel, the wireless masts, and the houses of town. He could see the car ferries lying at the Trumbo dock where he would go around to head up for the Garrison Bight. That old Willie, he thought. He was giving them hell. Wonder who those buzzards were. Damn if I don't feel plenty bad right now. I feel plenty dizzy. We did right to come in. We did right not to wait.

"Mr. Harry," said the nigger, "I'm sorry I couldn't help dump that stuff."

"Hell," said Harry, "ain't no nigger any good when he's shot. You're a all right nigger, Wesley."

Above the roar of the motors and the high, slapping rush of the boat through the water he felt a strange, hollow singing in his heart. He always felt this way coming home at the end of a trip. I hope they can fix that arm, he thought. I got a lot of use for that arm.

PART THREE
HARRY MORGAN
(Winter)

CHAPTER NINE

Albert Speaking

WE WERE all in there at Freddie's place and this tall thin lawyer comes in and says, "Where's Juan?"

"He ain't back yet," somebody said.

"I know he's back and I've got to see him."

"Sure, you tipped them off to him and you got him indicted and now you're going to defend him," Harry said. "Don't you come around here asking where he is. You probably got him in your pocket."

"Balls to you," said the lawyer. "I've got a job for him."

"Well, go look for him some place else," Harry said. "He ain't here."

"I've got a job for him, I tell you," the lawyer said.

"You ain't got a job for anybody. All you are is poison."

Just then the old man with the long gray hair over the back of his collar who sells the rubber goods specialties comes in for a quarter of a pint and Freddy pours it out for him and he corks it up and scuttles back across the street with it.

"What happened to your arm?" the lawyer asked Harry. Harry has the sleeve pinned up to the shoulder.

"I didn't like the look of it so I cut it off," Harry told him.

"You and who else cut it off?"

"Me and a doctor cut it off," Harry said. He had been drinking and he was getting a little along with it. "I held still and he cut it off. If they cut them off for being in other people's pockets you wouldn't have no hands nor no feet."

"What happened to it that they had to cut it off?" the lawyer asked him.

"Take it easy," Harry told him.

"No, I'm asking you. What happened to it and where were you?"

"Go bother somebody else," Harry told him. "You know where I was and you know what happened. Keep your mouth shut and don't bother me."

"I want to talk to you," the lawyer told him.

"Then talk to me."

"No, in back."

"I don't want to talk to you. No good ever comes of you. You're poison."

"I've got something for you. Something good."

"All right. I'll listen to you once," Harry told him. "What's it about? Juan?"

"No. Not about Juan."

They went back behind the bend of the bar into

where the booths are and they were gone quite a while. During the time they were gone Big Lucie's daughter came in with that girl from their place that she's always around with, and they sat at the bar and had a coca-cola.

"They tell me they ain't going to let no girls out on the streets after six o'clock at night and no girls in any of the places," Freddy says to Big Lucie's daughter.

"That's what they say."

"It's getting to be a hell of a town," Freddy says.

"Hell of a town is right. You just walk outside to get a sandwich and a coca-cola and they arrest you and fine you fifteen dollars."

"That's all they pick on now," says Big Lucie's daughter. "Any kind of sporting people. Anybody with any sort of a cheerful outlook."

"If something don't happen to this town pretty quick things are going to be bad."

Just then Harry and the lawyer came back out and the lawyer said, "You'll be out there then?"

"Why not bring them here?"

"No. They don't want to come in. Out there."

"All right," Harry said and stepped up to the bar and the lawyer went on out.

"What will you have, Al?" he asked me.

"Bacardi."

"Give us two bacardis, Freddy." Then he turned to me and said, "What are you doing now, Al?"

"Working on the relief."

"What doing?"

"Digging the sewer. Taking the old streetcar rails up."

"What do you get?"

"Seven and a half."

"A week?"

"What did you think?"

"How do you drink in here?"

"I wasn't till you asked me," I told him. He edged over a little towards me. "You want to make a trip?"

"Depends on what it is."

"We'll talk about that."

"All right."

"Come on out in the car," he said. "So long, Freddy." He breathed a little fast the way he did when he's been drinking and I walked up along where the street had been tore up, where we'd been working all day, to the corner where his car was. "Get in," he said.

"Where are we going?" I asked him.

"I don't know," he said. "I'm going to find out."

We drove up Whitehead Street and he didn't say anything and at the head of the street he turned to the left and we drove across the head of town to White Street and out on it to the beach. All the time Harry didn't say anything and we turned onto the sand road and drove along it to the boulevard. Out on the boulevard he pulled the car over to the edge of the sidewalk and stopped.

"Some strangers want to charter my boat to make a trip," he said.

"The customs got your boat tied up."

"The strangers don't know that."

"What kind of a trip?"

"They say they want to carry somebody over that has to go to Cuba to do some business and can't come in by the plane or boat. Bee-lips was telling me."

"Do they do that?"

"Sure. All the time since the revolution. It sounds all right. Plenty of people go that way."

"What about the boat."

"We'll have to steal the boat. You know they ain't got her fixed so I can't start her."

"How you going to get her out of the sub-base?"

"I'll get her out."

"How're we coming back?"

"I'll have to figure that. If you don't want to go, say so."

"I'd just as soon go if there's any money in it."

"Listen," he said. "You're making seven dollars and a half a week. You got three kids in school that are hungry at noon. You got a family that their bellies hurt and I give you a chance to make a little money."

"You ain't said how much money. You got to have money for taking chances."

"There ain't much money in any kind of chances

now, Al," he said. "Look at me. I used to make thirty-five dollars a day right through the season taking people out fishing. Now I get shot and lose an arm, and my boat, running a lousy load of liquor that's worth hardly as much as my boat. But let me tell you, my kids ain't going to have their bellies hurt and I ain't going to dig sewers for the government for less money than will feed them. I can't dig now anyway. I don't know who made the laws but I know there ain't no law that you got to go hungry."

"I went out on strike against those wages," I told him.

"And you come back to work," he said. "They said you were striking against charity. You always worked, didn't you? You never asked anybody for charity."

"There ain't any work," I said. "There ain't any work at living wages anywhere."

"Why?"

"I don't know."

"Neither do I," he said. "But my family is going to eat as long as anybody eats. What they're trying to do is starve you Conchs out of here so they can burn down the shacks and put up apartments and make this a tourist town. That's what I hear. I hear they're buying up lots, and then after the poor people are starved out and gone somewhere else to starve some more they're going to come in and make it into a beauty spot for tourists."

"You talk like a radical," I said.

"I ain't no radical," he said. "I'm sore. I been sore a long time."

"Losing your arm don't make you feel better."

"The hell with my arm. You lose an arm you lose an arm. There's worse things than lose an arm. You've got two arms and you've got two of something else. And a man's still a man with one arm or with one of those. The hell with it," he says. "I don't want to talk about it." Then after a minute he says, "I got those other two still." Then he started the car and said, "Come on, we'll go see these fellows."

We rode along the boulevard with the breeze blowing and a few cars going past and the smell of dead sea grass on the cement where the waves had gone over the seawall at high tide, Harry driving with his left arm. I always liked him all right and I'd gone in a boat with him plenty of times in the old days, but he was changed now since he lost his arm and that fellow down visiting from Washington made an affidavit that he saw the boat unloading liquor that time, and the customs seized her. When he was in a boat he always felt good and without his boat he felt plenty bad. I think he was glad of an excuse to steal her. He knew he couldn't keep her but maybe he could make a piece of money with her while he had her. I needed money bad enough but I didn't want to get in any trouble. I said to him, "You know I don't want to get in any real trouble, Harry."

"What worse trouble you going to get in than

you're in now?" he said. "What the hell worse trouble is there than starving?"

"I'm not starving," I said. "What the hell you always talking about starving for?"

"Maybe you're not, but your kids are."

"Cut it out," I said. "I'll work with you but you can't talk that way to me."

"All right," he said. "But be sure you want the job. I can get plenty of men in this town."

"I want it," I said. "I told you I want it."

"Then cheer up."

"You cheer up," I said. "You're the only one that's talking like a radical."

"Aw, cheer up," he said. "None of you Conchs has any guts."

"Since when ain't you a Conch?"

"Since the first good meal I ever ate." He was mean talking now, all right, and since he was a boy he never had no pity for nobody. But he never had no pity for himself either.

"All right," I said to him.

"Take it easy," he said. Ahead of us I could see the lights of this place.

"We're going to meet them here," Harry said. "Keep your mouth buttoned up."

"The hell with you."

"Aw, take it easy," Harry said as we turned into the runway and drove around to the back of the place.

He was a bully and he was bad spoken but I always liked him all right.

We stopped the car in back of this place and went into the kitchen where the man's wife was cooking at a stove. "Hello, Freda," Harry said to her. "Where's Bee-lips?"

"He's right in there, Harry. Hello, Albert."

"Hello, Miss Richards," I said. I knew her ever since she used to be in jungle town, but two or three of the hardest working married women in town used to be sporting women and this was a hard working woman, I tell you that. "Your folks all well?" she asked me.

"They're all fine."

We went on through the kitchen and into this back room. There was Bee-lips, the lawyer, and four Cubans with him, sitting at a table.

"Sit down," said one of them in English. He was a tough looking fellow, heavy, with a big face and a voice deep in his throat, and he had been drinking plenty you could see. "What's your name?"

"What's yours?" said Harry.

"All right," said this Cuban. "Have it your own way. Where's the boat?"

"She's down at the yacht basin," Harry said.

"Who's this?" the Cuban asked him, looking at me.

"My mate," Harry said. The Cuban was looking me over and the other Cubans were looking us both over. "He looks hungry," the Cuban said and laughed. The others didn't laugh. "You want a drink?"

"All right," Harry said.

"What? Bacardi?"

"Whatever you're drinking," Harry told him.

"Does your mate drink?"

"I'll have one," I said.

"Nobody asked you yet," the big Cuban said. "I just asked if you drank."

"Oh, cut it out, Roberto," one of the other Cubans, a young one, not much more than a kid, said. "Can't you do anything without getting nasty?"

"What do you mean nasty? I just asked if he drinks. If you hire somebody don't you ask if he drinks?"

"Give him a drink," said the other Cuban. "Let's talk business."

"What you want for the boat, big boy?" the deep-voiced Cuban called Roberto asked Harry.

"Depends on what you want to do with her," Harry said.

"Take the four of us to Cuba."

"Where in Cuba?"

"Cabañas. Close to Cabañas. Down the coast from Mariel. You know where it is?"

"Sure," said Harry. "Just take you there?"

"That's all. Take us there and put us ashore."

"Three hundred dollars."

"Too much. What if we charter you by the day and guarantee you two weeks' charter?"

"Forty dollars a day and you put up fifteen hundred dollars for if anything happens to the boat. Do I have to clear it?"

"No."

"You pay for the gas and oil," Harry told them.

"We'll give you two hundred dollars to take us over there and put us ashore."

"No."

"How much do you want?"

"I told you."

"That's too much."

"No, it isn't," Harry told him. "I don't know who you are. I don't know what your business is and I don't know who shoots at you. I got to cross the Gulf twice in the winter time. Anyway I'm risking my boat. I'll carry you for two hundred and you can put up a thousand for a guaranty nothing happens to the boat."

"That's reasonable," Bee-lips told them. "That's more than reasonable."

The Cubans started talking in Spanish. I couldn't understand them but I knew Harry could.

"All right," the big one, Roberto, said. "When can you start?"

"Any time tomorrow night."

"Maybe we don't want to go until the night after," one of them said.

"That's O.K. with me," Harry said. "Only let me know in time."

"Is your boat in good shape?"

"Sure," said Harry.

"She is a nice looking boat," the young one of them said.

"Where did you see her?"

"Mr. Simmons, the lawyer here, showed her to me."

"Oh," said Harry.

"Have a drink," said another of the Cubans. "Have you been to Cuba much?"

"A few times."

"Speak Spanish?"

"I never learned it," Harry said.

I saw Bee-lips, the lawyer, look at him, but he is so crooked himself that he's always more pleased if people aren't telling the truth. Just like when he came in to speak to Harry about this job he couldn't speak to him straight. He had to pretend he wanted to see Juan Rodriguez, who is a poor stinking Gallego that would steal from his own mother that Bee-lips has got indicted again so he can defend him.

"Mr. Simmons speaks good Spanish," the Cuban said.

"He's got an education."

"Can you navigate?"

"I can go and I can come."

"You're a fisherman?"

"Yes, sir," said Harry.

"How do you fish with one arm?" the big faced one asked.

"You just fish twice as fast," Harry told him. "Did you want to see me about anything else?"

"No."

They were all talking Spanish together. "Then I'll go," said Harry.

"I'll let you know about the boat," Bee-lips told Harry.

"There's some money got to be put up," Harry said.

"We'll do that tomorrow."

"Well, good night," Harry told them.

"Good night," said the young pleasant speaking one. The big faced one didn't say anything. There were two others with faces like Indians that hadn't said anything at all any of the time except to talk in Spanish to the big faced one.

"I'll see you later on," Bee-lips said.

"Where?"

"At Freddy's."

We went out and through the kitchen again and Freda said, "How's Marie, Harry?"

"She's fine now," Harry told her. "She's feeling good now," and we went out the door. We got in the car and he drove back to the boulevard and didn't say anything at all. He was thinking about something all right.

"Should I drop you home?"

"All right."

"You live out on the county road now?"

"Yes. What about the trip?"

"I don't know," he said. "I don't know whether there's going to be any trip. See you tomorrow."

He drops me in front of where we live and I go on in and I haven't got the door open before my old woman is giving me hell for staying out and drinking and being late to the meal. I ask her how I can drink with no money and she says I must be running a credit. I ask her who she thinks will give me credit when I'm working on the relief and she says to keep my rummy breath away from her and sit down to the table. So I sit down. The kids are all gone to the diamond ball game and I sit there at the table and she brings the supper and won't speak to me.

CHAPTER TEN

Harry

I DON'T want to fool with it but what choice have I got? They don't give you any choice now. I can let it go; but what will the next thing be? I didn't ask for any of this and if you've got to do it you've got to do it. Probably I shouldn't take Albert. He's dumb but he's straight and he's a good man in a boat. He doesn't spook too easy but I don't know whether I ought to take him. But I can't take no rummy nor no nigger. I got to have somebody I can depend on. If we make it I'll see he gets a share. But I can't tell him or he wouldn't go into it and I got to have somebody by me. It would be better alone, anything is better alone but I don't think I can handle it alone. It would be much better alone. Albert is better off if he don't know anything about it. The only thing is Bee-lips. There's Bee-lips that will know about everything. Still they must have thought about that. They must figure on that. Do you suppose Bee-lips is so dumb he won't know that's what they will do? I wonder. Of course maybe that isn't what they figure to do. Maybe they aren't going to do any such thing.

But it's natural that's what they would do and I heard that word. If they do it they'll have to do it just when it closes or they'll have the coast guard plane down from Miami. It's dark now at six. She can't fly it down under an hour. Once it's dark they're all right. Well, if I'm going to carry them I got to figure out about the boat. She won't be hard to get out but if I take her out tonight and they find she's gone they'll maybe find her. Anyway there will be a big fuss. Tonight's the only time I've got to get her out though. I can take her out with the tide and I can hide her. I can see what she needs if she needs anything, if they've taken off anything. But I got to fill gas and water. I got a hell of a busy night all right. Then when I've got her hid Albert will have to bring them in a speed boat. Maybe Walton's. I can hire her. Or Bee-lips can hire her. That's better. Bee-lips can help me get the boat out tonight. Bee-lips is the one. Because sure as hell they've figured about Bee-lips. They've got to have figured about Bee-lips. Suppose they figure about me and Albert. Did any of them look like sailors? Did any of them seem like they were sailors? Let me think? Maybe. The pleasant one, maybe. Possibly him, that young one. I have to find out about that because if they figure on doing without Albert or me from the start there's no way. Sooner or later they will figure on us. But in the Gulf you got time. And I'm figuring all the time. I've got to think right all the time. I can't make a

mistake. Not a mistake. Not once. Well, I got something to think about now all right. Something to do
and something to think about besides wondering
what the hell's going to happen. Besides wondering
what's going to happen to the whole damn thing.
Once they put it up. Once you're playing for it. Once
you got a chance. Instead of just watching it all go to
hell. With no boat to make a living with. That Bee-
lips. He don't know what he's into. He ain't got any
idea what this is going to be like. I hope he shows up
pretty soon down at Freddy's. I got plenty to do
tonight. I better get something to eat.

CHAPTER ELEVEN

IT WAS about nine-thirty when Bee-lips came into the place. You could see they had given him plenty out at Richard's because when he drinks it makes him cocky and he came in plenty cocky.

"Well, big shot," he says to Harry.

"Don't big shot me," Harry told him.

"I want to talk to you, big shot."

"Where? Back in your office?" Harry asked him.

"Yes, back there. Anybody back there, Freddy?"

"Not since that law. Say, how long are they going to have that six o'clock business?"

"Why don't you retain me to do something about it?" Bee-lips says.

"Retain you hell," Freddy tells him. And the two of them go back there where the booths and the cases with the empty bottles are.

There was one electric light on in the ceiling and Harry looked in all the booths where it was dark and saw there was no one.

"Well," he said.

"They want it for late day after tomorrow afternoon," Bee-lips told him.

"What they going to do?"

"You speak Spanish," Bee-lips said.

"You didn't tell them that though?"

"No. I'm your pal. You know that."

"You'd rat on your own mother."

"Cut it out. Look at what I'm letting you in on."

"When did you get tough?"

"Listen, I need the money. I've got to get out of here. I'm all washed up here. You know that, Harry."

"Who don't know that?"

"You know how they've been financing this revolution with kidnapping and the rest of it."

"I know."

"This is the same sort of thing. They're doing it for a good cause."

"Yeah. But this is here. This is where you were born. You know everybody works there."

"Nothing's going to happen to anybody."

"With those guys?"

"I thought you had *cojones*."

"I got *cojones*. Don't you worry about my *cojones*. But I'm figuring on keeping on living here."

"I'm not," Bee-lips said.

Jesus, thought Harry. He's said it himself.

"I'm going to get out," Bee-lips said.

"When are you going to get the boat out?"

"Tonight."

"Who's going to help you?"

"You."

"Where you going to put her?"

"Where I always put her."

There was nothing difficult about getting the boat out. It was as simple as Harry had figured it. The night watchman made his rounds on the hour and the rest of the time he was at the outer gate of the old Navy Yard. They came into the basin in a skiff, cut her loose on the ebb tide and she went out herself with the skiff towing her. Outside, while she drifted in the channel, Harry checked the motors and found all they had done was disconnect the distributor heads. He checked the gas and found she had close to a hundred and fifty gallons. They hadn't syphoned any out of the tanks and she had what he had left coming across that last time. He had filled her up before they started and she had burned very little because they had to come across so slow in the heavy seas.

"I've got gas at the house in the tank," he told Bee-lips. "I can take one load of demijohns out with me in the car and Albert can bring another if we need it. I'm going to put her up in the creek right where it crosses the road. They can come out in a car."

"They wanted you to be right at the Porter Dock."

"How can I lay there with this boat?"

"You can't. But I don't think they'll want to do any car driving."

"Well, we'll put her there tonight and I can fill and do what needs to be done and then shift her. You can hire a speed boat to bring them out. I got to put her up there now. I got plenty to do. You scull in and drive out to the bridge and pick me up. I'll be on the road there in about two hours. I'll leave her and come out to the road."

"I'll pick you up," Bee-lips told him, and Harry with the motors throttled down so that she moved quietly through the water, swung her around and towed the skiff close in to where the riding light of the cable schooner showed. He threw the clutches out and held the skiff while Bee-lips got in.

"In about two hours," he said.

"All right," said Bee-lips.

Sitting on the steering seat, moving ahead slowly in the dark, keeping well out from the lights at the head of the docks, Harry thought, Bee-lips is doing some work for his money all right. Wonder how much he thinks he is going to get? I wonder how he ever hooked up with those guys. There's a smart kid who had a good chance once. He's a good lawyer, too. But it made me cold to hear him say it himself. He put his mouth on his own self all right. It's funny how a man can mouth something. When I heard him mouth himself it scared me.

CHAPTER TWELVE

WHEN HE came in the house he did not turn on the light but took off his shoes in the hall and went up the bare stairs in his stocking feet. He undressed and got into bed wearing only his undershirt, before his wife woke. In the dark she said, "Harry?" and he said, "Go to sleep, old woman."

"Harry, what's the matter?"

"Going to make a trip."

"Who with?"

"Nobody. Albert maybe."

"Whose boat?"

"I got the boat again."

"When?"

"Tonight."

"You'll go to jail, Harry."

"Nobody knows I've got her."

"Where is she?"

"Hid."

Lying still in the bed he felt her lips on his face and searching for him and then her hand on him and he rolled over against her close.

"Do you want to?"

"Yes. Now."

"I was asleep. Do you remember when we'd do it asleep?"

"Listen, do you mind the arm? Don't it make you feel funny?"

"You're silly. I like it. Any that's you I like. Put it across there. Put it along there. Go on. I like it, true."

"It's like a flipper on a loggerhead."

"You ain't no loggerhead. Do they really do it three days? Coot for three days?"

"Sure. Listen, be quiet. We'll wake the girls."

"They don't know what I've got. They won't never know what I've got. Ah, Harry. That's it. Ah, you honey."

"Wait."

"I don't want no wait. Come on. That's it. That's where. Listen, did you ever do it with a nigger wench?"

"Sure."

"What's it like?"

"Like nurse shark."

"You're funny. Harry, I wish you didn't have to go. I wish you didn't ever have to go. Who's the best you ever did it with?"

"You."

"You lie. You always lie to me. There. There. There."

"No. You're the best."

"I'm old."

"You'll never be old."

"I've had that thing."

"That don't make no difference when a woman's any good."

"Go ahead. Go ahead now. Put the stump there. Hold it there. Hold it. Hold it now. Hold it."

"We're making too much noise."

"We're whispering."

"I got to get out before it's daylight."

"You go to sleep. I'll get you up. When you come back we'll have a time. We'll go to a hotel up in Miami like we used to. Just like we used to. Some place where they never seen either of us. Why couldn't we go to New Orleans?"

"Maybe," Harry said. "Listen Marie, I got to go to sleep now."

"We'll go to New Orleans?"

"Why not? Only I got to go to sleep."

"Go to sleep. You're my big honey. Go on to sleep. I'll wake you. Don't you worry."

He went to sleep with the stump of his arm out wide on the pillow, and she lay for a long time look-ing at him. She could see his face in the street light through the window. I'm lucky, she was thinking. Those girls. They don't know what they'll get. I know what I've got and what I've had. I've been a lucky woman. Him saying like a loggerhead. I'm glad it was a arm and not a leg. I wouldn't like him to have lost a leg. Why'd he have to lose that arm? It's

funny though, I don't mind it. Anything about him I
don't mind. I've been a lucky woman. There ain't no
other men like that. People ain't never tried them
don't know. I've had plenty of them. I've been lucky
to have him. Do you suppose those turtles feel like we
do? Do you suppose all that time they feel like that?
Or do you suppose it hurts the she? I think of the
damndest things. Look at him, sleeping just like a
baby. I better stay awake so as to call him. Christ, I
could do that all night if a man was built that way. I'd
like to do it and never sleep. Never, never, no, never.
No, never, never, never. Well, think of that, will you.
Me at my age. I ain't old. He said I was still good.
Forty-five ain't old. I'm two years older than him.
Look at him sleep. Look at him asleep there like a
kid.

Two hours before it was daylight they were out at
the gas tank in the garage filling and corking demijohns and putting them in the back of the car. Harry
wore a hook strapped to his right arm and shifted
and lifted the wicker-covered demijohns handily.

"You don't want no breakfast?"

"When I come back."

"Don't you want your coffee?"

"You got it?"

"Sure. I put it on when we came out."

"Bring it out."

She brought it out and he drank it in the dark sitting at the wheel of the car. She took the cup and put it on the shelf in the garage.

"I'm coming with you to help you handle the jugs," she said.

"All right," he told her and she got in beside him, a big woman, long legged, big handed, big hipped, still handsome, a hat pulled down over her bleached blonde hair. In the dark and the cold of the morning they drove out the county road through the mist that hung heavy over the flat.

"What you worried about, Harry?"

"I don't know. I'm just worried. Listen, are you letting your hair grow out?"

"I thought I would. The girls have been after me."

"The hell with them. You keep it like it is."

"Do you really want me to?"

"Yes," he said. "That's the way I like it."

"You don't think I look too old?"

"You look better than any of them."

"I'll fix it up then. I can make it blonder if you like it."

"What have the girls got to say about what you do?" Harry said. "They got no business to bother you."

"You know how they are. You know young girls are that way. Listen, if you make a good trip, we'll go to New Orleans, should we?"

"Miami."

"Well, Miami anyway. And we'll leave them here."

"I got some trip to make first."

"You aren't worried, are you?"

"No."

"You know I lay awake almost four hours just thinking about you."

"You're some old woman."

"I can think about you any time and get excited."

"Well, we got to fill this gas now," Harry told her.

CHAPTER THIRTEEN

AT TEN o'clock in the morning in Freddy's place Harry was standing in against the bar with four or five others, and two customs men had just left. They had asked him about the boat and he had said he did not know anything about it.

"Where were you last night?" one of them asked.

"Here and at home."

"How late were you here?"

"Until the place shut."

"Anybody see you here?"

"Plenty of people," Freddy said.

"What's the matter?" Harry asked them. "Do you think I'd steal my own boat? What would I do with it?"

"I just asked you where you were," the Customs House officer said. "Don't get plugged."

"I'm not plugged," Harry said. "I was plugged back when they seized the boat without any proof she carried liquor."

"There was an affidavit sworn to," the customs man said. "It wasn't my affidavit. You know the man that made it."

"All right," said Harry. "Only don't say I'm

plugged at you asking me. I'd rather you had her tied up. Then I got a chance to get her back. What chance I got if she's stolen?"

"None, I guess," said the customs man.

"Well, go peddle your papers," Harry said.

"Don't get snotty," said the customs man, "or I'll see you get something to be snotty about."

"After fifteen years," said Harry.

"You haven't been snotty fifteen years."

"No, and I haven't been in jail either."

"Well, don't be snotty or you will be."

"Take it easy," Harry said. Just then this goofy Cuban that drives a taxi came in with a fellow from the plane and Big Rodger says to him,

"Hayzooz, they tell me you had a baby."

"Yes, *sir*," says Hayzooz very proudly.

"When did you get married?" Rodger asked him.

"Lasta month. Montha for last. You come the wedding?"

"No," said Rodger. "I didn't come the wedding."

"You missa something," said Hayzooz. "You missa damn fine wedding. Whas a matta you no come?"

"You didn't ask me."

"Oh, yes," said Hayzooz. "I forget. I didn't ask you. . . . You get what you want?" he asked the stranger.

"Yes. I think so. Is that the best price you have on Bacardi?"

"Yes, sir," Freddy told him. "That's the real carta del oro."

"Listen Hayzooz, what makes you think that's your baby?" Rodger asks him. "That's not your baby."

"What you mean not my baby? What you mean? By God, I no let you talk like that! What you mean not my baby? You buy the cow you no get the calf? That's my baby. My God, yes. My baby. Belong to me. Yes, *sir!*"

He goes out with the stranger and the bottle of Bacardi and the laugh is on Rodger all right. That Hayzooz is a character all right. Him and that other Cuban, Sweetwater.

Just then in comes Bee-lips the lawyer, and he says to Harry, "The customs just went out to take your boat."

Harry looked at him and you could see the murder come in his face. Bee-lips went on in this same tone without any expression in it. "Somebody saw it in the mangroves from the top of one of those high WPA trucks and called up from where they're building the camp out at Boca Chica to the Customs House. I just saw Herman Frederichs. He told me."

Harry didn't say anything, but you could see the killing go out of his face and his eyes came open natural again. Then he said to Bee-lips, "You hear everything, don't you?"

"I thought you'd like to know," Bee-lips said in that same expressionless voice.

"It's none of my concern," Harry said. "They ought to take better care of a boat than that."

The two of them stood there at the bar and neither one said anything until Big Rodger and the two or three others had drifted out. Then they went in the back.

"You're poison," Harry said. "Everything you touch is poison."

"Is it my fault a truck could see it? You picked the place. You hid your own boat."

"Shut up," Harry said. "Did they ever have high trucks like that before? That's the last chance I had to make any honest money. That's the last chance I got to go in a boat where there's any money."

"I let you know as soon as it happened."

"You're like a buzzard."

"Cut it out," Bee-lips said. "They want to go late this afternoon now."

"The hell they do."

"They're getting nervous about something."

"What time do they want to go?"

"Five o'clock."

"I'll get a boat. I'll carry them to hell."

"That isn't a bad idea."

"Don't mouth that now. Keep your mouth off my business."

"Listen, you big murdering slob," said Bee-lips, "I try to help you out and get you in on some-thing——"

"And all you do is poison me. Shut up. You're poison to anybody that ever touched you."

"Cut it out, you bully."

"Take it easy," Harry said. "I got to think. All I've done is think one thing out and I got it thought out and now I got to think out something else."

"Why don't you let me help you?"

"You come here at twelve o'clock and bring that money to put up for the boat."

As they came out Albert came up to the place and went up to Harry.

"I'm sorry, Albert, I can't use you," Harry said. He had thought it out that far already.

"I'd go cheap," Albert said.

"I'm sorry," Harry said. "I got no need for you now."

"You won't get a good man for what I'll go for," Albert said.

"I'm going by myself."

"You don't want to make a trip like that alone," Albert said.

"Shut up," said Harry. "What do you know about it? Do they teach you my business on the relief?"

"Go to hell," said Albert.

"Maybe I will," said Harry. Anybody looking at him could tell he was thinking plenty fast and he did not want to be bothered.

"I'd like to go," Albert said.

"I can't use you," Harry said. "Let me alone, will you?"

Albert went out and Harry stood there at the bar looking at the nickel machine, the two dime machines and the quarter machine and at the picture of Custer's Last Stand on the wall as though he'd never seen them.

"That was a good one Hayzooz told Big Rodger about the baby, wasn't it?" Freddy said to him, putting some coffee glasses in the bucket of soapy water.

"Give me a package of Chesterfields," Harry said to him. He held the package under the flap of his arm and opened it at one corner, took a cigarette out and put it in his mouth, then dropped the package in his pocket and lit the cigarette.

"What shape's your boat in, Freddy?" he asked.

"I just had her on the ways," Freddy said. "She's in good shape."

"Do you want to charter her?"

"What for?"

"For a trip across."

"Not unless they put up the value of her."

"What's she worth?"

"Twelve hundred dollars."

"I'll charter her," Harry said. "Will you trust me on her?"

"No," Freddy told him.

"I'll put up the house as security."

"I don't want your house. I want twelve hundred bucks up."

"All right," Harry said.

"Bring around the money," Freddy told him.

"When Bee-lips comes in, tell him to wait for me," Harry said and went out.

CHAPTER FOURTEEN

OUT AT THE house Marie and the girls were having lunch.

"Hello Daddy," said the oldest girl. "Here's Daddy."

"What have you got to eat?" Harry asked.

"We've got a steak," Marie said.

"Somebody said they stole your boat, Daddy."

"They found her," Harry said.

Marie looked at him.

"Who found her?" she asked.

"The Customs."

"Oh, Harry," she said, full of pity.

"Isn't it better they found her, Daddy?" asked the second one of the girls.

"Don't talk while you're eating," Harry told her. "Where's my dinner? What you waiting for?"

"I'm bringing it."

"I'm in a hurry," Harry said. "You girls eat up and get out. I got to talk to your mother."

"Can we have some money to go to the show this aft, Daddy?"

"Why don't you go swimming. That's free."

"Oh, Daddy, it's too cold to go swimming, and we want to go to the show."

"All right," said Harry. "All right."

When the girls were out of the room he said to Marie, "Cut it up, will you?"

"Sure, Honey."

She cut the meat as for a small boy.

"Thanks," Harry said. "I'm a hell of a goddamn nuisance, ain't I? Those girls aren't much, are they?"

"No, Hon."

"Funny we couldn't get no boys."

"That's because you're such a man. That way it always comes out girls."

"I ain't no hell of a man," Harry said. "But listen, I'm going on a hell of a trip."

"Tell me about the boat."

"They saw it from a truck. A high truck."

"Shucks."

"Worse than that. Shit."

"Aw, Harry, don't talk like that in the house."

"You talk worse than that in bed sometimes."

"That's different. I don't like to hear shit at my own table."

"Oh, shit."

"Aw, Honey, you feel bad," Marie said.

"No," said Harry. "I'm just thinking."

"Well, you think it out. I got confidence in you."

"I got confidence. That's the only thing I have got."

"Do you want to tell me about it?"

"No. Only don't worry no matter what you hear."

"I won't worry."

"Listen, Marie. Go on up to the upstairs trap and bring me the Thompson gun and look in that wooden box with the shells and see all the clips are filled."

"Don't take that."

"I got to."

"Do you want any boxes of shells?"

"No. I can't load any clips. I got four clips."

"Honey, you aren't going on that kind of a trip?"

"I'm going on a bad trip."

"Oh, God," she said. "Oh, God, I wish you didn't have to do these things."

"Go on and get it and bring it down here. Get me some coffee."

"O.K.," said Marie. She leaned over the table and kissed him on the mouth.

"Leave me alone," Harry said. "I got to think."

He sat at the table and looked at the piano, the sideboard and the radio, the picture of September Morn, and the pictures of the cupids holding bows behind their heads, the shiny real-oak table and the shiny real-oak chairs and the curtains on the windows and he thought, What chance have I to enjoy my home? Why am I back to worse than where I started? It'll all be gone too if I don't play this right. The hell it will. I haven't got sixty bucks left outside of the house, but I'll get a stake out of this. Those damn girls. That's all that old woman and I could get with what we've got. Do you suppose the boys in her went before I knew her?

"Here it is," said Marie, carrying it by the web sling strap. "They're all full."

"I got to go," Harry said. He lifted the chunky weight of the dismounted gun in its oil-stained, canvas-web case. "Put it under the front seat of the car."

"Good-by," Marie said.

"Good-by, old woman."

"I won't worry. But please take care of yourself."

"Be good."

"Aw, Harry," she said and held him tight against her.

"Let me go. I ain't got no time."

He patted her on the back with his arm stump.

"You and your loggerhead flipper," she said. "Oh, Harry. Be careful."

"I got to go. Good-by, old woman."

"Good-by, Harry."

She watched him go out of the house, tall, wide-shouldered, flat-backed, his hips narrow, moving, still, she thought, like some kind of animal, easy and swift and not old yet, he moves so light and smooth-like, she thought, and when he got in the car she saw him blonde, with the sunburned hair, his face with the broad mongol cheek bones, and the narrow eyes, the nose broken at the bridge, the wide mouth and the round jaw, and getting in the car he grinned at her and she began to cry. "His goddamn face," she thought. "Everytime I see his goddamn face it makes me want to cry."

CHAPTER FIFTEEN

THERE WERE three tourists at the bar at Freddy's and Freddy was serving them. One was a very tall, thin, wide-shouldered man, in shorts, wearing thick-lensed spectacles, tanned, with small closely trimmed sandy mustache. The woman with him had her blonde curly hair cut short like a man's, a bad complexion, and the face and build of a lady wrestler. She wore shorts, too.

"Oh, nerts to you," she was saying to the third tourist, who had a rather swollen reddish face, a rusty-colored mustache, a white cloth hat with a green celluloid visor, and a trick of talking with a rather extraordinary movement of his lips as though he were eating something too hot for comfort.

"How charming," said the green-visored man. "I'd never heard the expression actually used in conversation. I thought it was an obsolete phrase, something one saw in print in—er—the funny papers but never heard."

"Nerts, nerts, double nerts to you," said the lady wrestler lady in a sudden access of charm, giving him the benefit of her pimpled profile.

"How beautiful," said the green-visored man.

"You put it so prettily. Isn't it from Brooklyn originally?"

"You mustn't mind her. She's my wife," the tall tourist said. "Have you two met?"

"Oh, nerts to him and double nerts to meeting him," said the wife. "How do you do?"

"Not so badly," the green-visored man said. "How do *you* do?"

"She does marvellously," the tall one said. "You ought to see her."

Just then Harry came in and the tall tourist's wife said, "Isn't he wonderful? That's what I want. Buy me that, Papa."

"Can I speak to you?" Harry said to Freddy.

"Certainly. Go right ahead and say anything you like," the tall tourist's wife said.

"Shut up, you whore," Harry said. "Come in the back, Freddy."

In the back was Bee-lips, waiting at the table.

"Hello, Big Boy," he said to Harry.

"Shut up," said Harry.

"Listen," Freddy said. "Cut it out. You can't get away with that. You can't call my trade names like that. You can't call a lady a whore in a decent place like this."

"A whore," said Harry. "Hear what she said to me?"

"Well, anyway, don't call her a name like that to her face."

"All right. You got the money?"

"Of course," said Bee-lips. "Why wouldn't I have the money? Didn't I say I'd have the money?"

"Let's see it."

Bee-lips handed it over. Harry counted ten hundred-dollar bills and four twenties.

"It should be twelve hundred."

"Less my commission," said Bee-lips.

"Come on with it."

"No."

"Come on."

"Don't be silly."

"You miserable little crut."

"You big bully," Bee-lips said. "Don't try to strong arm it away from me because I haven't got it here."

"I see," said Harry. "I should have thought of that. Listen Freddy. You've known me a long time. I know she's worth twelve hundred. This is a hundred and twenty short. Take it and take a chance on the hundred and twenty and the charter."

"That's three hundred and twenty dollars," Freddy said. It was a painful sum for him to name as a risk, and he sweated while he thought about it.

"I got a car and a radio in the house that's good for it."

"I can make out a paper on that," Bee-lips said.

"I don't want any paper," Freddy said. He sweat again and his voice was hesitant. Then he said, "All

right. I'll take a chance. But for Christ's sake be careful with the boat, will you Harry?"

"Like it was my own."

"You lost your own," said Freddy, still sweating,
his suffering now intensified by that memory.

"I'll take care of her."

"I'll put the money in my box in the bank," Freddy
said.

Harry looked at Bee-lips.

"That's a good place," he said, and grinned.

"Bartender," some one called from the front.

"That's you," Harry said.

"Bartender," came the voice again.

Freddy went out to the front.

"That man insulted me," Harry could hear the
high voice saying, but he was talking to Bee-lips.

"I'll be tied up to the dock there at the front of the
street. It isn't half a block."

"All right."

"That's all."

"All right, Big Shot."

"Don't you big shot me."

"However you like."

"I'll be there from four o'clock on."

"Anything else?"

"They got to take me by force, see? I know nothing about it. I'm just working on the engine. I got
nothing aboard to make a trip. I've hired her from
Freddy to go charter fishing. They've got to hold a

gun on me to make me start her and they've got to cut loose the lines."

"What about Freddy? You didn't hire her to go fishing from him."

"I'm going to tell Freddy."

"You better not."

"I'm going to."

"You better not."

"Listen, I've done business with Freddy since during the war. Twice I've been partners with him and we never had trouble. You know how much stuff I've handled for him. He's the only son-of-a-bitch in this town I *would* trust."

"I wouldn't trust anybody."

"*You* shouldn't. Not after the experiences you've had with yourself."

"Lay off me."

"All right. Go out and see your friends. What's *your* out?"

"They're Cubans. I met them out at the roadhouse. One of them wants to cash a certified check. What's wrong with that?"

"And you don't notice anything?"

"No. I tell them to meet me at the bank."

"Who drives them?"

"Some taxi."

"What's he supposed to think they are, violinists?"

"We'll get one that don't think. There's plenty of them that can't think in this town. Look at Hayzooz."

"Hayzooz is smart. He just talks funny."

"I'll have them call a dumb one."

"Get one hasn't any kids."

"They all got kids. Ever see a taxi driver without kids?"

"You are a goddamn rat."

"Well, I never killed anybody," Bee-lips told him.

"Nor you never will. Come on, let's get out of here. Just being with you makes me feel crummy."

"Maybe you are crummy."

"Can you get them from talking?"

"If you don't paper your mouth."

"Paper yours then."

"I'm going to get a drink," Harry said.

Out in front the three tourists sat on their high stools. As Harry came up to the bar the woman looked away from him to register disgust.

"What will you have?" asked Freddy.

"What's the lady drinking," Harry asked.

"A Cuba Libre."

"Then give me a straight whiskey."

The tall tourist with the little sandy mustache and the thick-lensed glasses leaned his large, straight-nosed face over toward Harry and said, "Say, what's the idea of talking that way to my wife?"

Harry looked him up and down and said to Freddy, "What kind of a place you running?"

"What about it?" the tall one said.

"Take it easy," Harry said to him.

"You can't pull that with me."

"Listen," Harry said. "You came down here to get well and strong, didn't you? Take it easy." And he went out.

"I should have hit him, I guess," the tall tourist said. "What do you think, dear?"

"I wish I was a man," his wife said.

"You'd go a long way with that build," the green-visored man said into his beer.

"What did you say," the tall one asked.

"I said you could find out his name and address and write him a letter telling him what you think of him."

"Say, what's your name, anyway? What are you doing, kidding me?"

"Just call me Professor MacWalsey."

"My name's Laughton," the tall one said. "I'm a writer."

"I'm glad to meet you," Professor MacWalsey said. "Do you write often?"

The tall man looked around him. "Let's get out of here, dear," he said. "Everybody is either insulting or nuts."

"It's a strange place," said Professor MacWalsey. "Fascinating, really. They call it the Gibraltar of America and it's three hundred and seventy-five miles south of Cairo, Egypt. But this place is the only part of it I've had time to see yet. It's a fine place though."

"I see you're a professor all right," the wife said. "You know, I like you."

"I like you too, darling," Professor MacWalsey said. "But I have to go now."

He got up and went out to look for his bicycle.

"Everybody is nuts here," the tall man said. "Should we have another drink, dear?"

"I liked the professor," the wife said. "He had a sweet manner."

"That other fellow——"

"Oh, he had a beautiful face," the wife said. "Like a Tartar or something. I wish he hadn't been insulting. He looked kind of like Ghengis Khan in the face. Gee, he was big."

"He had only one arm," her husband said.

"I didn't notice," the wife said. "Should we have another drink? I wonder who'll come in next!"

"Maybe Tamerlane," the husband said.

"Gee, you're educated," the wife said. "But that Ghengis Khan one would do me. Why did the professor like to hear me say nerts?"

"I don't know, dear," Laughton, the writer, said. "I never did."

"He seemed to like me for what I really am," the wife said. "My, he was nice."

"You'll probably see him again."

"Any time you come in here you'll see *him*," Freddy said. "He lives in here. He's been here for two weeks now."

"Who's the other one who speaks so rude?"

"Him? Oh, he's a fellow from around here."

"What does he do?"

"Oh, a little of everything," Freddy told her. "He's a fisherman."

"How did he lose his arm?"

"I don't know. He got it hurt some way."

"Gee, he's beautiful," the wife said.

Freddy laughed. "I heard him called a lot of things but I never heard him called that."

"Don't you think he has a beautiful face?"

"Take it easy, lady," Freddy told her. "He's got a face like a ham with a broken nose on it."

"My, men are stupid," the wife said. "He's my dream man."

"He's a bad-dream man," Freddy said.

All this time the writer sat there with a sort of stupid look on his face except when he'd look at his wife admiringly. Any one would have to be a writer or a F.E.R.A. man to have a wife look like that, Freddy thought. God, isn't she awful?

Just then in came Albert.

"Where's Harry?"

"Down at the dock."

"Thanks," said Albert.

He went out and the wife and the writer kept on sitting there and Freddy stood there worrying about the boat and thinking how his legs hurt from standing up all day. He had put a grating over the cement but it didn't seem to do much good. His legs ached all the time. Still he was doing a good business, as good as anybody in town and with less overhead. That woman was goofy all right. And what kind of a man was it would pick out a woman like that to live with? Not even with your eyes shut, thought Freddy. Not with a borrowed. Still they were drinking mixed drinks. Expensive drinks. That was something.

"Yes, sir," he said. "Right away."

A tanned-faced, sandy-haired, well-built man wearing a striped fisherman's shirt and khaki shorts came in with a very pretty dark girl who wore a thin, white wool sweater and dark blue slacks.

"If it isn't Richard Gordon," said Laughton, standing up, "with the lovely Miss Helen."

"Hello, Laughton," said Richard Gordon. "Did you see anything of a rummy professor around here?"

"He just went out," said Freddy.

"Do you want a vermouth, sweetheart?" Richard Gordon asked his wife.

"If you do," she said. Then said, "Hello," to the two Laughtons. "Make mine two parts of French to one Italian, Freddy."

She sat on a high stool with her legs tucked under her and looked out at the street. Freddy looked at her admiringly. He thought she was the prettiest stranger in Key West that winter. Prettier even than the famous beautiful Mrs. Bradley. Mrs. Bradley was getting a little big. This girl had a lovely Irish face, dark hair that curled almost to her shoulders and smooth clear skin. Freddy looked at her brown hand holding the glass.

"How's the work?" Laughton asked Richard Gordon.

"I'm going all right," Gordon said. "How are you doing?"

"James won't work," Mrs. Laughton said. "He just drinks."

"Say, who is this Professor MacWalsey?" Laughton asked.

"Oh, he's some sort of professor of economics I think, on a sabbatical year or something. He's a friend of Helen's."

"I like him," said Helen Gordon.

"I like him, too," said Mrs. Laughton.

"I liked him first," Helen Gordon said happily.

"Oh, you can have him," Mrs. Laughton said. "You good little girls always get what you want."

"That's what makes us so good," said Helen Gordon.

"I'll have another vermouth," said Richard Gordon. "Have a drink?" he asked the Laughtons.

"Why not," said Laughton. "Say, are you going to that big party the Bradleys are throwing tomorrow?"

"Of course he is," said Helen Gordon.

"I like her, you know," said Richard Gordon. "She interests me both as a woman and as a social phenomenon."

"Gee," said Mrs. Laughton. "You can talk as educated as the professor."

"Don't strut your illiteracy, dear," said Laughton.

"Do people go to bed with a social phenomenon?" asked Helen Gordon, looking out the door.

"Don't talk rot," said Richard Gordon.

"I mean is it part of the homework of a writer?" Helen asked.

"A writer has to know about everything," Richard Gordon said. "He can't restrict his experience to conform to bourgeois standards."

"Oh," said Helen Gordon. "And what does a writer's wife do?"

"Plenty, I guess," Mrs. Laughton said. "Say, you ought to have seen the man who was just in here and insulted me and James. He was terrific."

"I should have hit him," Laughton said.

"He was really terrific," said Mrs. Laughton.

"I'm going home," said Helen Gordon. "Are you coming, Dick?"

"I thought I'd stay down town a while," Richard Gordon said.

"Yes?" said Helen Gordon, looking in the mirror behind Freddy's head.

"Yes," Richard Gordon said.

Freddy, looking at her, figured that she was going

to cry. He hoped it wouldn't happen in the place.

"Don't you want another drink?" Richard Gordon asked her.

"No." She shook her head.

"Say, what's the matter with you?" asked Mrs. Laughton. "Aren't you having a good time?"

"A dandy time," said Helen Gordon. "But I think I'd better go home just the same."

"I'll be back early," Richard Gordon said.

"Don't bother," she told him. She went out. She hadn't cried. She hadn't found John MacWalsey either.

CHAPTER SIXTEEN

DOWN AT THE dock Harry Morgan had driven up alongside of where the boat lay, seen there was no one around, lifted the front seat of his car, skidded the flat, web, oil-heavy case out and dropped it down into the cockpit of the launch.

He got in himself and opened the engine hatch and put the machine-gun case below out of sight. He turned on the gas valves and started both engines. The starboard engine ran smoothly after a couple of minutes, but the port engine missed on the second and fourth cylinders and he found the plugs were cracked, looked for some new plugs, but couldn't find them.

"Got to get plugs and fill gas," he thought.

Below with the engines, he opened the machine-gun case and fitted the stock to the gun. He found two pieces of fan belting and four screws, and cutting slits in the belting rigged a sling to hold the gun under the cockpit floor to the left of the hatch; just over the port engine. It lay there, cradled easily, and he shoved a clip from the four held in the web pockets in the case up into the gun. Kneeling between the two engines he reached up to take the gun. There were only two movements to make. First unhook the strap of belting that passed around the receiver just behind the bolt. Then pull the gun out of the other loop. He tried it and it came easily one-handed. He pushed the little lever all the way over from semi-automatic to automatic and made sure the safety was on. Then he fastened it up again. He could not figure out where to put the extra clips; so he shoved the case under a gas tank below, where he could reach it, with the butts of the clips lying toward his hand. If I go down a time first after we're under-way, I can put a couple in my pocket, he thought. Be better not to have it on but something might jar the damn thing off.

He stood up. It was a fine clear afternoon, pleasant, not cold, with a light north breeze. It was a nice after-noon all right. The tide was running out and there were two pelicans sitting on the piling at the edge of the channel. A grunt fishing boat, painted dark green, chugged past on the way around to the fish market, the Negro fisherman sitting in the stern holding the tiller. Harry looked out across the water, smooth with the wind blowing with the tide, gray blue in the afternoon sun, out to the sandy island formed when the channel was dredged where the shark camp had been located. There were white gulls flying over the island.

"Be a pretty night," Harry thought. "Be a nice night to cross."

He was sweating a little from being down around the engines, and he straightened up and wiped his face with a piece of waste.

There was Albert on the dock.

"Listen, Harry," he said. "I wish you'd carry me."

"What's the matter with you now?"

"They're only going to give us three days a week on the relief now. I just heard about it this morning. I got to do something."

"All right," said Harry. He had been thinking again. "All right."

"That's good," said Albert. "I was afraid to go home to see my old woman. She gave me hell this noon like it was me had laid off the relief."

"What's the matter with your old woman?" asked Harry cheerfully. "Why don't you smack her?"

"You smack her," Albert said. "I'd like to hear what she'd say. She's some old woman to talk."

"Listen, Al," Harry told him. "Take my car and this and go around to the Marine Hardware and get six metric plugs like this one. Then go get a 20-cent piece of ice and a half a dozen mullets. Get two cans of coffee, four cans of cornbeef, two loaves of bread, some sugar and two cans of condensed milk. Stop at the Sinclair and tell them to come down here and put in a hundred and fifty gallons. Get back as soon as you can and change the number two and the number four plugs in the port engine counting back from the flywheel. Tell them I'll be back to pay for the gas. They can wait or find me at Freddy's. Can you remember all that? We're taking a party out tarponing and fishing them tomorrow."

"It's too cold for tarpon," Albert said.

"The party says no," Harry told him.

"Hadn't I better get a dozen mullets?" Albert asked. "In case the jacks tear 'em up? There's plenty jacks now in those channels."

"Well, make it a dozen. But get back inside an hour and have the gas filled."

"Why you want to put in so much gas?"

"We may be running early and late and not have time to fill."

"What's become of those Cubans that wanted to be carried?"

"Haven't heard anything more from them."

"That was a good job."

"This is a good job too. Come on, get going."

"What am I going to be working for?"

"Five bucks a day," said Harry. "If you don't want it don't take it."

"All right," said Albert. "Which plugs was it?"

"The number two and the number four counting back from the flywheel," Harry told him. Albert nodded his head. "I guess I can remember," he said. He got into the car and made a turn in it and went off up the street.

From where Harry stood in the boat he could see the brick and stone building and the front entrance of the First State Trust and Savings Bank. It was just a block down at the foot of the street. He couldn't see the side entrance. He looked at his watch. It was a little after two o'clock. He shut the engine hatch and climbed up on the dock. Well, now it comes off or it doesn't, he thought. I've done what I can now. I'll go up and see Freddy and then I'll come back and wait. He turned to the right as he left the dock and walked down a back street so that he would not pass the bank.

CHAPTER SEVENTEEN

IN AT FREDDY'S he wanted to tell him about it but he couldn't. There wasn't anybody in the bar and he sat on a stool and wanted to tell him, but it was impossible. As he was ready to tell him he knew Freddy would not stand for it. In the old days, maybe, yes, but not now. Maybe not in the old days either. It wasn't until he thought of telling it to Freddy that he realized how bad it was. I could stay right here, he thought, and there wouldn't be anything. I could stay right here and have a few drinks and get hot and I wouldn't be in it. Except there's my gun on the boat. But nobody knows it's mine except the old woman. I got it in Cuba on a trip the time when I peddled those others. Nobody knows I've got it. I could stay here now and I'd be out of it. But what the hell would they eat on? Where's the money coming from to keep Marie and the girls? I've got no boat, no cash, I got no education. What can a one-armed man work at? All I've got is my *cojones* to peddle. I could stay right here and have say five more drinks and it would all be over. It would be too late then. I could just let it all slide and do nothing.

"Give me a drink," he said to Freddy.

"Sure."

I could sell the house and we could rent until I got some kind of work. What kind of work? No kind of work. I could go down to the bank and squeal now and what would I get? Thanks. Sure. Thanks. One bunch of Cuban government bastards cost me my arm shooting at me with a load when they had no need to and another bunch of U. S. ones took my boat. Now I can give up my home and get thanks. No thanks. The hell with it, he thought. I got no choice in it.

He wanted to tell Freddy so there would be some one knew what he was doing. But he couldn't tell him because Freddy wouldn't stand for it. He was making good money now. There was nobody much in the daytime, but every night the place was full until two o'clock. Freddy wasn't in a jam. He knew he wouldn't stand for it. I have to do it alone, he thought, with that poor bloody Albert. Christ, he looked hungrier than ever down at the dock. There were Conchs that would starve to death before they'd steal all right. Plenty in this town with their bellies hollering right now. But they'd never make a move. They'd just starve a little every day. They started starving when they were born; some of them.

"Listen, Freddy," he said. "I want a couple of quarts."

"Of what?"

"Bacardi."

"O.K."

"Pull the corks, will you? You know I wanted to charter her to take some Cubans over."

"That's what you said."

"I don't know when they'll be going. Maybe tonight. I haven't heard."

"She's ready to go anytime. You've got a nice night if you cross tonight."

"They said something about going fishing this afternoon."

"She's got tackle on board if the pelicans haven't stole it off her."

"It's still there."

"Well, make a good trip," Freddy said.

"Thanks. Give me another one, will you?"

"Of what?"

"Whiskey."

"I thought you were drinking Bacardi."

"I'll drink that if I get cold going across."

"You'll cross with this breeze astern all the way," said Freddy. "I'd like to cross tonight."

"It'll be a pretty night all right. Let me have another, will you?"

Just then in came the tall tourist and his wife.

"If it isn't my dream man," she said, and sat down on the stool beside Harry.

He took one look at her and stood up.

"I'll be back, Freddy," he said. "I'm going down

to the boat in case that party wants to go fishing."

"Don't go," the wife said. "Please don't go."

"You're comical," Harry said to her and he went out.

Down the street Richard Gordon was on his way to the Bradleys' big winter home. He was hoping Mrs. Bradley would be alone. She would be. Mrs. Bradley collected writers as well as their books but Richard Gordon did not know this yet. His own wife was on her way home walking along the beach. She had not run into John MacWalsey. Perhaps he would come by the house.

CHAPTER EIGHTEEN

ALBERT was on board the boat and the gas was loaded.

"I'll start her up and try how those two cylinders hit," Harry said. "You got the things stowed?"

"Yes."

"Cut some baits then."

"You want a wide bait?"

"That's right. For tarpon."

Albert was on the stern cutting baits and Harry was at the wheel warming up the motors when he heard a noise like a motor backfiring. He looked down the street and saw a man come out of the bank. He had a gun in his hand and he came running. Then he was out of sight. Two more men came out carrying leather brief cases and guns in their hands and ran in the same direction. Harry looked at Albert busy cutting baits. The fourth man, the big one, came out of the bank door as he watched, holding a Thompson gun in front of him, and as he backed out of the door the siren in the bank rose in a long breath-holding shriek and Harry saw the gun muzzle jump-jump-jump-jump and heard the bop-bop-bop-bop, small and hollow sounding in the wail of the siren. The man turned and ran, stopping to fire once more at the bank door, and as Albert stood up in the stern saying, "Christ, they're robbing the bank. Christ, what can we do?" Harry heard the Ford taxi coming out of the side street and saw it careening up onto the dock.

There were three Cubans in the back and one beside the driver.

"Where's the boat?" yelled one in Spanish.

"There, you fool," said another.

"That's not the boat."

"That's the captain."

"Come on. Come on for Christ sake."

"Get out," said the Cuban to the driver. "Get your hands up."

As the driver stood beside the car he put a knife inside his belt and ripping it toward him cut the belt and slit his pants almost to the knee. He yanked the trousers down. "Stand still," he said. The two Cubans with the valises tossed them into the cockpit of the launch and they all came tumbling aboard.

"Geta going," said one. The big one with the machine-gun poked it into Harry's back.

"Come on, Cappie," he said. "Let's go."

"Take it easy," said Harry. "Point that some place else."

"Cast off those lines," the big one said. "You!" to Albert.

"Wait a minute," Albert said. "Don't start her. These are the bank robbers."

The biggest Cuban turned and swung the Thompson gun and held it on Albert. "Hey, don't! Don't!" Albert said. "Don't!"

The burst was so close to his chest that the bullets whocked like three slaps. Albert slid down on his knees, his eyes wide, his mouth open. He looked like he was still trying to say, "Don't!"

"You don't need no mate," the big Cuban said. "You one-armed son-of-a-bitch." Then in Spanish, "Cut those lines with that fish knife." And in English, "Come on. Let's go."

Then in Spanish, "Put a gun against his back!" and in English, "Come on. Let's go. I'll blow your head off."

"We'll go," said Harry.

One of the Indian-looking Cubans was holding a pistol against the side his bad arm was on. The muzzle almost touched the hook.

As he swung her out, spinning the wheel with his good arm, he looked astern to watch the clearance past the piling, and saw Albert on his knees in the stern, his head slipped sidewise now, in a pool of it. On the dock was the Ford taxi, and the fat driver in his underdrawers, his trousers around his ankles, his hands above his head, his mouth open as wide as Albert's. There was still no one coming down the street.

The pilings of the dock went past as she came out of the basin and then he was in the channel passing the lighthouse dock.

"Come on. Hook her up," the big Cuban said. "Make some time."

"Take that gun away," Harry said. He was thinking, I could run her on Crawfish bar, but sure as hell that Cuban would plug me.

"Make her go," said the big Cuban. Then, in Spanish, "Lie down flat, everybody. Keep the captain covered." He lay down himself in the stern, pulling Albert flat down into the cockpit. The other three all lay flat in the cockpit now. Harry sat on the steering seat. He was looking ahead steering out the channel, past the opening into the sub-base now, with the notice board to yachts and the green blinker, out away from the jetty, past the fort now, past the red blinker; he looked back. The big Cuban had a green box of shells out of his pocket and was filling clips. The gun lay by his side and he was filling clips without looking at them, filling by feel, looking back over the stern. The others were all looking astern except the one that was watching him. This one, one of the two Indian-looking ones, motioned with his pistol for him to look ahead. No boat had started after them yet. The engines were running smoothly and they were going with the tide. He noticed the heavy slant seawards of the buoy he passed, with the current swirling at its base.

There are two speedboats that could catch us, Harry was thinking. One, Ray's, is running the mail from Matecumbe. Where is the other? I saw her a couple of days ago on Ed. Taylor's ways, he checked. That was the one I thought of having Bee-lips hire. There's two more, he remembered now. One the State Road Department has up along the keys. The other's laid up in the Garrison Bight. How far are we now? He looked back to where the fort was well astern, the red-brick building of the old Postoffice starting to show up above the Navy yard buildings and the yellow hotel building now dominating the short skyline of the town. There was the cove at the fort, and the lighthouse showed above the houses that strung out toward the big winter hotel. Four miles anyway, he thought. There they come, he thought. Two white fishing boats were rounding the break-water and heading out toward him. They can't do ten, he thought. It's pitiful.

The Cubans were chattering in Spanish.

"How fast you going, Cappie?" the big one said, looking back from the stern.

"About twelve," Harry said.

"What can those boats do?"

"Maybe ten."

They were all watching them now, even the one who was supposed to keep him, Harry, covered. But what can I do? He thought. Nothing to do yet.

The two white boats got no larger.

"Look at that, Roberto," said the nice-speaking one.

"Where?"

"Look!"

A long way back, so far you could hardly see it, a little spout rose in the water.

"They're shooting at us," the pleasant-speaking one said. "It's silly."

"For Christ's sake," the big-faced one said. "At three miles."

"Four," thought Harry. "All of four."

Harry could see the tiny spouts rise on the calm surface but he could not hear the shots.

"Those Conchs are pitiful," he thought. "They're worse. They're comical."

"What government boat is there, Cappie?" asked the big-faced one looking away from the stern.

"Coast guard."

"What can she make?"

"Maybe twelve."

"Then we're O.K. now."

Harry did not answer.

"Aren't we O.K. then?"

Harry said nothing. He was keeping the rising, widening spire of Sand Key on his left and the stake on little Sand Key shoals showed almost abeam to starboard. In ten more minutes they would be past the reef.

"What's the matter with you? Can't you talk?"

"What did you ask me?"

"Is there anything can catch us now?"

"Coast guard plane," said Harry.

"We cut the telephone wire before we came in town," the pleasant-speaking one said.

"You didn't cut the wireless, did you?" Harry asked.

"You think the plane can get here?"

"You got a chance of her until dark," Harry said.

"What do you think, Cappy?" asked Roberto, the big-faced one.

Harry did not answer.

"Come on, what do you think?"

"What did you let that son-of-a-bitch kill my mate for?" Harry said to the pleasant-speaking one who was standing beside him now looking at the compass course.

"Shut up," said Roberto. "Kill you, too."

"How much money you get?" Harry asked the pleasant-speaking one.

"We don't know. We haven't counted it yet. It isn't ours, anyway."

"I guess not," said Harry. He was past the light now and he put her on 225°, his regular course for Havana.

"I mean we do it not for ourselves. For a revolutionary organization."

"You kill my mate for that, too?"

"I am very sorry," said the boy. "I cannot tell you how badly I feel about that."

"Don't try," said Harry.

"You see," the boy said, speaking quietly, "this

man Roberto is bad. He is a good revolutionary but a bad man. He kills so much in the time of Machado he gets to like it. He thinks it is funny to kill. He kills in a good cause, of course. The best cause." He looked back at Roberto who sat now in one of the fishing chairs in the stern, the Thompson gun across his lap, looking back at the white boats which were, Harry saw, much smaller now.

"What you got to drink?" Roberto called from the stern.

"Nothing," Harry said.

"I drink my own, then," Roberto said. One of the other Cubans lay on one of the seats built over the gas tanks. He looked seasick already. The other was obviously seasick too, but still sitting up.

Looking back, Harry saw a lead-colored boat, now clear of the fort, coming up on the two white boats.

"There's the coast guard boat," he thought. "She's pitiful too."

"You think the seaplane will come?" the pleasant-spoken boy asked.

"Be dark in half an hour," Harry said. He settled on the steering seat. "What you figure on doing? Killing me?"

"I don't want to," the boy said. "I hate killing."

"What you doing?" Roberto, who sat now with a pint of whiskey in his hand, asked. "Making friends with the captain? What you want to do? Eat at the captain's table?"

"Take the wheel," Harry said to the boy. "See the course? Two twenty-five." He straightened up from the stool and went aft.

"Let me have a drink," Harry said to Roberto. "There's your coast guard boat but she can't catch us."

He had abandoned anger, hatred and any dignity as luxuries, now, and had started to plan.

"Sure," said Roberto. "She can't catch us. Look at those seasick babies. What you say? You want a drink? You got any other last wishes, Cappie?"

"You're some kidder," Harry said. He took a long drink.

"Go easy!" Roberto protested. "That's all there is."

"I got some more," Harry told him. "I was just kidding you."

"Don't kid me," said Roberto suspiciously.

"Why should I try?"

"What you got?"

"Bacardi."

"Bring it out."

"Take it easy," Harry said. "Why do you get so tough?"

He stepped over Albert's body as he walked forward. As he came to the wheel he looked at the compass. The boy was about twenty-five degrees off and the compass dial was swinging. He's no sailor, Harry thought. That gives me more time. Look at the wake.

The wake ran in two bubbling curves toward where the light, astern now, showed brown, conical and thinly latticed on the horizon. The boats were almost out of sight. He could just see a blur where the wireless masts of the town were. The engines were running smoothly. Harry put his head below and reached for one of the bottles of Bacardi. He went aft with it. At the stern he took a drink, then handed the bottle to Roberto. Standing, he looked down at Albert and he felt sick inside. The poor hungry bastard, he thought.

"What's the matter? He scare you?" the big-faced Cuban asked.

"What you say we put him over?" Harry said. "No sense to carry him."

"O.K.," said Roberto. "You got good sense."

"Take him under the arms," said Harry. "I'll take the legs." Roberto laid the Thompson gun down on the wide stern and leaning down lifted the body by the shoulders.

"You know the heaviest thing in the world is a dead man," he said. "You ever lift a dead man before, Cappie?"

"No," said Harry. "You ever lift a big dead woman?"

Roberto pulled the body up onto the stern. "You're a tough fellow," he said. "What do you say we have a drink?"

"Go ahead," said Harry.

"Listen, I'm sorry I killed him," Roberto said. "When I kill you I feel worse."

"Cut out talking that way," Harry said. "What do you want to talk that way for?"

"Come on," said Roberto. "Over he goes."

As they leaned over and slid the body up and over the stern, Harry kicked the machine gun over the edge. It splashed at the same time Albert did, but while Albert turned over twice in the white, churned, bubbling back-suction of the propellor wash before sinking, the gun went straight down.

"That's better, eh?" Roberto said. "Make it ship-shape." Then as he saw the gun was gone, "Where is it? What did you do with it?"

"With what?"

"The *ametralladora!*" going into Spanish in excitement.

"The what?"

"You know what."

"I didn't see it."

"You knocked it off the stern. Now I'll kill you, *now.*"

"Take it easy," said Harry. "What the hell you going to kill me about?"

"Give me a gun," Roberto said to one of the seasick Cubans in Spanish. "Give me a gun quick!"

Harry stood there, never having felt so tall, never having felt so wide, feeling the sweat trickle from under his armpits, feeling it go down his flanks.

"You kill too much," he heard the seasick Cuban say in Spanish. "You kill the mate. Now you want to kill the captain. Who's going to get us across?"

"Leave him alone," said the other. "Kill him when we get over."

"He knocked the machine gun overboard," Roberto said.

"We got the money. What you want a machine gun for now? There's plenty of machine guns in Cuba."

"I tell you, you make a mistake if you don't kill him now, I tell you. Give me a gun."

"Oh, shut up. You're drunk. Every time you're drunk you want to kill somebody."

"Have a drink," said Harry looking out across the gray swell of the Gulf Stream where the round red sun was just touching the water. "Watch that. When she goes all the way under it'll turn bright green."

"The hell with that," said the big-faced Cuban. "You think you got away with something."

"I'll get you another gun," said Harry. "They only cost forty-five dollars in Cuba. Take it easy. You're all right now. There ain't any coast guard plane going to come now."

"I'm going to kill you," Roberto said, looking him over. "You did that on purpose. That's why you got me to lift on that."

"You don't want to kill me," Harry said. "Who's going to take you across?"

"I ought to kill you now."

"Take it easy," said Harry. "I'm going to look at the engines."

He opened the hatch, got down in, screwed down the grease cups on the two stuffing boxes, felt of the motors, and with his hand touched the butt of the Thompson gun. Not yet, he thought. No, better not yet. Christ, that was lucky. What the hell difference does it make to Albert when he's dead? Saves his old woman to bury him. That big-faced bastard. That big-faced murdering bastard. Christ, I'd like to take him now. But I better wait.

He stood up, climbed out and shut the hatch.

"How you doing?" he said to Roberto. He put his hand on the fat shoulder. The big-faced Cuban looked at him and did not say anything.

"Did you see it turn green?" Harry asked.

"The hell with you," Roberto said. He was drunk but he was suspicious and, like an animal, he knew how wrong something had gone.

"Let me take her a while," Harry said to the boy at the wheel. "What's your name?"

"You can call me Emilio," said the boy.

"Go below and you'll find something to eat," Harry said. "There's bread and cornbeef. Make coffee if you want."

"I don't want any."

"I'll make some later," Harry said. He sat at the wheel, the binnacle light on now, holding her on the point easily in the light following sea, looking out at the night coming on the water. He had no running lights on.

It would be a pretty night to cross, he thought, a pretty night. Soon as the last of that afterglow is gone I've got to work her east. If I don't, we'll sight the glare of Havana in another hour. In two, anyway. Soon as he sees the glare it may occur to that son-of-a-bitch to kill me. That was lucky getting rid of that gun. Damn, that was lucky. Wonder what that Marie's having for supper. I guess she's plenty worried. I guess she's too worried to eat. Wonder how much money those bastards have got. Funny they don't count it. If that ain't a hell of a way to raise money for a revolution. Cubans are a hell of a people.

That's a mean boy, that Roberto. I'll get him tonight. I get him no matter how the rest of it comes out. That won't help that poor damned Albert though. It made me feel bad to dump him like that. I don't know what made me think of it.

He lit a cigarette and smoked in the dark.

I'm doing all right, he thought. I'm doing better than I expected. The kid is a kind of nice kid. I wish I could get those other two on the same side. I wish there was some way to bunch them. Well, I'll have to do the best I can. Easier I can make them take it beforehand the better. Smoother everything goes the better.

"Do you want a sandwich?" the boy asked.

"Thanks," said Harry. "You give one to your partner?"

"He's drinking. He won't eat," the boy said.

"What about the others?"

"Seasick," the boy said.

"It's a nice night to cross," Harry said. He noticed the boy did not watch the compass so he kept letting her go off to the east.

"I'd enjoy it," the boy said. "If it wasn't for your mate."

"He was a good fellow," said Harry. "Did any one get hurt at the bank?"

"The lawyer. What was his name, Simmons."

"Get killed?"

"I think so."

So, thought Harry. Mr. Bee-lips. What the hell did he expect? How could he have thought he wouldn't get it? That comes from playing at being tough. That comes from being too smart too often. Mr. Bee-lips. Good-by, Mr. Bee-lips.

"How he come to get killed?"

"I guess you can imagine," the boy said. "That's very different from your mate. I feel badly about that. You know he doesn't mean to do wrong. It's just what that phase of the revolution has done to him."

"I guess he's probably a good fellow," Harry said, and thought, Listen to what my mouth says. God damn it, my mouth will say anything. But I got to try to make a friend of this boy in case——

"What kind of revolution do you make now?" he asked.

"We are the only true revolutionary party," the boy said. "We want to do away with all the old politicians, with all the American imperialism that strangles us, with the tyranny of the army. We want to start clean and give every man a chance. We want to end the slavery of the *guajiros,* you know, the peasants, and divide the big sugar estates among the people that work them. But we are not Communists."

Harry looked up from the compass card at him.

"How you coming on?" he asked.

"We just raise money now for the fight," the boy said. "To do that we have to use means that later we would never use. Also we have to use people we would not employ later. But the end is worth the means. They had to do the same thing in Russia. Stalin was a sort of brigand for many years before the revolution."

He's a radical, Harry thought. That's what he is, a radical.

"I guess you've got a good program," he said, "if you're out to help the working man. I was out on strike plenty times in the old days when we had the cigar factories in Key West. I'd have been glad to do whatever I could if I'd known what kind of outfit you were."

"Lots of people would help us," the boy said. "But because of the state the movement is in at present we can't trust people. I regret the necessity for the present phase very much. I hate terrorism. I also feel very badly about the methods for raising the necessary money. But there is no choice. You do not know how bad things are in Cuba."

"I guess they're plenty bad," Harry said.

"You can't know how bad they are. There is an absolutely murderous tyranny that extends over every little village in the country. Three people cannot be together on the street. Cuba has no foreign enemies and doesn't need any army, but she has an army of twenty-five thousand now, and the army, from the corporals up, suck the blood from the nation. Every one, even the private soldiers, are out to make their fortunes. Now they have a military reserve with every kind of crook, bully and informer of the old days of Machado in it, and they take anything the army does not bother with. We have to get rid of the army before anything can start. Before we were ruled by clubs. Now we are ruled by rifles, pistols, machine guns, and bayonets."

"It sounds bad," Harry said, steering, and letting her go off to the eastward.

"You cannot realize how bad it is," the boy said. "I love my poor country and I would do anything,

anything to free it from this tyranny we have now. I do things I hate. But I would do things I hate a thousand times more."

I want a drink, Harry was thinking. What the hell do I care about his revolution. F—— his revolution. To help the working man he robs a bank and kills a fellow works with him and then kills that poor damned Albert that never did any harm. That's a working man he kills. He never thinks of that. With a family. It's the Cubans run Cuba. They all double-cross each other. They sell each other out. They get what they deserve. The hell with their revolutions. All I got to do is make a living for my family and I can't do that. Then he tells me about his revolution. The hell with his revolution.

"It must be bad, all right," he said to the boy. "Take the wheel a minute, will you? I want to get a drink."

"Sure," said the boy. "How should I steer?"

"Two twenty-five," Harry said.

It was dark now and there was quite a swell this far out in the Gulf Stream. He passed the two sea-sick Cubans lying out on the seats and went aft to where Roberto sat in the fishing chair. The water was racing past the boat in the dark. Roberto sat with his feet in the other fishing chair that was turned toward him.

"Let me have some of that," Harry said to him.

"Go to hell," said the big-faced man thickly. "This is mine."

"All right," said Harry, and went forward to get the other bottle. Below in the dark, with the bottle under the flap of his right arm, he pulled the cork that Freddy had drawn and re-inserted and took a drink.

Now's as good as any time, he said to himself. No sense waiting now. Little boy's spoke his piece. The big-faced bastard drunk. The other two seasick. It might as well be now.

He took another drink and the Bacardi warmed and helped him but he felt cold and hollow all around his stomach still. His whole insides were cold.

"Want a drink?" he asked the boy at the wheel.

"No, thanks," the boy said. "I don't drink." Harry could see him smile in the binnacle light. He was a nice-looking boy all right. Pleasant talking, too.

"I'll take one," he said. He swallowed a big one but it could not warm the dank cold part that had spread from his stomach to all over the inside of his chest now. He put the bottle down on the cockpit door.

"Keep her on that course," he said to the boy. "I'm going to have a look at the motors."

He opened the hatch and stepped down. Then locked the hatch up with a long hook that set into a hole in the flooring. He stooped over the motors, with his one hand felt the water manifold, the cylinders, and put his hand on the stuffing boxes. He tightened the two grease cups a turn and a half each. Quit stalling, he said to himself. Come on, quit stalling. Where're your balls now? Under my chin, I guess, he thought.

He looked out of the hatch. He could almost touch the two seats over the gas tanks where the seasick men lay. The boy's back was toward him, sitting on the high stool, outlined clearly by the binnacle light. Turning, he could see Roberto sprawled in the chair in the stern, silhouetted against the dark water.

Twenty-one to a clip is four bursts of five at the most, he thought. I got to be light-fingered. All right. Come on. Quit stalling, you gutless wonder. Christ, what I'd give for another one. Well, there isn't any other one now. He reached his left hand up, unhooked the length of belting, put his hand around the trigger guard, pushed the safety all the way over with his thumb and pulled the gun out. Squatting in the engine pit he sighted carefully on the base of the back of the boy's head where it outlined against the light from the binnacle.

The gun made a big flame in the dark and the shells rattled against the lifted hatch and onto the engine. Before the slump of the boy's body fell from the stool he had turned and shot into the figure on the left bunk, holding the jerking, flame-stabbing gun

almost against the man, so close he could smell it
burn his coat; then swung to put a burst into the
other bunk where the man was sitting up, tugging at
his pistol. He crouched low now and looked astern.
The big-faced man was gone out of the chair. He
could see both chairs silhouetted. Behind him the boy
lay still. There wasn't any doubt about him. On one
bunk a man was flopping. On the other, he could see
with the corner of his eye, a man lay half over the
gunwale, fallen over on his face.

Harry was trying to locate the big-faced man in
the dark. The boat was going in a circle now and the
cockpit lightened a little. He held his breath and
looked. That must be him where it was a little darker
on the floor in the corner. He watched it and it
moved a little. That was him.

The man was crawling toward him. No, toward
the man who lay half overboard. He was after his
gun. Crouching low, Harry watched him move until
he was absolutely sure. Then he gave him a burst.
The gun lighted him on hands and knees, and, as the
flame and the bot-bot-bot-bot stopped, he heard him
flopping heavily.

"You son-of-a-bitch," said Harry. "You big-faced
murdering bastard."

All the cold was gone from around his heart now
and he had the old hollow, singing feeling and he
crouched low down and felt under the square, wood-
crated gas tank for another clip to put in the gun.

He got the clip, but his hand was cold-drying wet.

Hit the tank, he said to himself. I've got to cut the engines. I don't know where that tank cuts.

He pressed the curved lever, dropped the empty clip, shoved in the fresh one, and climbed up and out of the cockpit.

As he stood up, holding the Thompson gun in his left hand, looking around before shutting the hatch with the hook on his right arm, the Cuban who had lain on the port bunk and had been shot three times through the left shoulder, two shots going into the gas tank, sat up, took careful aim, and shot him in the belly.

Harry sat down in a backward lurch. He felt as though he had been struck in the abdomen with a club. His back was against one of the iron-pipe supports of the fishing chairs and while the Cuban shot at him again and splintered the fishing chair above his head, he reached down, found the Thompson gun, raised it carefully, holding the forward grip with the hook and rattled half of the fresh clip into the man who sat leaning forward, calmly shooting at him from the seat. The man was down on the seat in a heap and Harry felt around on the cockpit floor until he could find the big-faced man, who lay face down, felt for his head with the hook on his bad arm, hooked it around, then put the muzzle of the gun against the head and touched the trigger. Touching the head, the gun made a noise like hitting a pumpkin with a club. Harry put down the gun and lay on his side on the cockpit floor.

"I'm a son-of-a-bitch," he said, his lips against the planking. I'm a gone son-of-a-bitch now. I got to cut the engines or we'll all burn up, he thought. I got a chance still. I got a kind of a chance. Jesus Christ. One thing to spoil it. One thing to go wrong. God damn it. Oh, God *damn* that Cuban bastard. Who'd have thought I hadn't got him?

He got on his hands and knees and letting one side of the hatch over the engines slam down, crawled over it forward to where the steering stool was. He pulled up on it, surprised to find how well he could move, then suddenly feeling faint and weak as he stood erect, he leaned forward with his bad arm resting on the compass and cut the two switches. The engines were quiet and he could hear the water against her sides. There was no other sound. She swung into the trough of the little sea the north wind had raised and began to roll.

He hung against the wheel, then eased himself onto the steering stool, leaning against the chart table. He could feel the strength drain out of him in a steady faint nausea. He opened his shirt with his good hand and felt the hole with the base of the palm of his hand, then fingered it. There was very little bleeding. All inside, he thought. I better lie down and give it a chance to quiet.

The moon was up now and he could see what was in the cockpit.

Some mess, he thought, some hell of a mess.

Better get down before I fall down, he thought and he lowered himself down to the cockpit floor.

He lay on his side and then, as the boat rolled, the moonlight came in and he could see everything in the cockpit clearly.

It's crowded, he thought. That's what it is, it's crowded. Then, he thought, I wonder what she'll do. I wonder what Marie will do? Maybe they'll pay her the rewards. God damn that Cuban. She'll get along, I guess. She's a smart woman. I guess we would all have gotten along. I guess it was nuts all right. I guess I bit off too much more than I could chew. I shouldn't have tried it. I had it all right up to the end. Nobody'll know how it happened. I wish I could do something about Marie. Plenty money on this boat. I don't even know how much. Anybody be O.K. with that money. I wonder if the coast guard will pinch it. Some of it, I guess. I wish I could let the old woman know what happened. I wonder what she'll do? I don't know. I guess I should have got a job in a filling station or something. I should have quit trying to go in boats. There's no honest money going in boats any more. If the bitch wouldn't only roll. If she'd only quit rolling. I can feel all that slopping back and forth inside. Me. Mr. Bee-lips and Albert. Everybody that had to do with it. These bastards too. It must be an unlucky business. Some unlucky business. I guess what a man like me ought to do is run something like a filling station. Hell, I couldn't run no filling station. Marie, she'll run something. She's too old to peddle her hips now. I wish this bitch wouldn't roll. I'll just have to take it easy. I got to take it as easy as I can. They say if you don't drink water and lay still. They say especially if you don't drink water.

He looked at what the moonlight showed in the cockpit.

Well, I don't have to clean her up, he thought. Take it easy. That's what I got to do. Take it easy. I've got to take it as easy as I can. I've got sort of a chance. If you lay still and don't drink any water.

He lay on his back and tried to breathe steadily. The launch rolled in the Gulf Stream swell and Harry Morgan lay on his back in the cockpit. At first he tried to brace himself against the roll with his good hand. Then he lay quietly and took it.

CHAPTER NINETEEN

THE NEXT MORNING in Key West Richard Gordon was on his way home from a visit to Freddy's Bar where he had gone to ask about the bank robbery. Riding his bicycle, he passed a heavy-set, big, blue-eyed woman, with bleached-blonde hair showing under her old man's felt hat, hurrying across the road, her eyes red from crying. Look at that big ox, he thought. What do you suppose a woman like that thinks about? What do you suppose she does in bed? How does her husband feel about her when she gets that size? Who do you suppose he runs around with in this town? Wasn't she an appalling looking woman? Like a battleship. Terrific.

He was almost home now. He left his bicycle on the front porch and went in the hallway, closing the front door the termites had tunnelled and riddled.

"What did you find out, Dick?" his wife called from the kitchen.

"Don't talk to me," he said. "I'm going to work. I have it all in my head."

"That's fine," she said. "I'll leave you alone."

He sat down at the big table in the front room. He was writing a novel about a strike in a textile factory.

In today's chapter he was going to use the big woman with the tear-reddened eyes he had just seen on the way home. Her husband when he came home at night hated her, hated the way she had coarsened and grown heavy, was repelled by her bleached hair, her too big breasts, her lack of sympathy with his work as an organizer. He would compare her to the young, firm-breasted, full-lipped little Jewess that had spoken at the meeting that evening. It was good. It was, it could be easily, terrific, and it was true. He had seen, in a flash of perception, the whole inner life of that type of woman.

Her early indifference to her husband's caresses. Her desire for children and security. Her lack of sympathy with her husband's aims. Her sad attempts to simulate an interest in the sexual act that had become actually repugnant to her. It would be a fine chapter.

The woman he had seen was Harry Morgan's wife, Marie, on her way home from the sheriff's office.

CHAPTER TWENTY

FREDDY WALLACE'S boat, the *Queen Conch,* 34 feet long, with a V number out of Tampa, was painted white; the forward deck was painted a color called Frolic green and the inside of the cockpit was painted Frolic green. The top of the house was painted the same color. Her name and home port, Key West, Fla., were painted in black across her stern. She was not equipped with outriggers and had no mast. She was equipped with glass windshields, one of which, that forward of the wheel, was broken. There were a number of fresh, wood-splintered holes in the newly painted planking of her hull. Splintered patches could be seen on both sides of her hull about a foot below the gunwale and a little forward of the center of the cockpit. There was another group of these splintered places almost at the water line on the starboard side of the hull opposite the aft stanchion that supported her house or awning. From the lower of these holes something dark had dripped and hung in ropy lines against the new paint of her hull.

She drifted broadside to the gentle north wind about ten miles outside of the north-bound tanker lanes, gay looking in her fresh white and green, against the dark, blue Gulf Stream water. There were patches of sun-yellowed Sargasso weed floating in the water near her that passed her slowly in the current going to the north and east, while the wind overcame some of the launch's drift as it set her steadily further out into the stream. There was no sign of life on her although the body of a man showed, rather inflated looking, above the gunwale, lying on a bench over the port gasoline tank and, from the long seat alongside the starboard gunwale, a man seemed to be leaning over to dip his hand into the sea. His head and arms were in the sun and at the point where his fingers almost touched the water, there was a school of small fish, about two inches long, oval-shaped, golden-colored, with faint purple stripes, that had deserted the gulf weed to take shelter in the shade the bottom of the drifting launch made in the water, and each time anything dripped down into the sea, these fish rushed at the drop and pushed and milled until it was gone. Two gray sucker fish about eighteen inches long swam round and round the boat in the shadow in the water, their slit mouths on the tops of their flat heads opening and shutting; but they did not seem to comprehend the regularity of the drip the small fish fed on and were as likely to be on the far side of the launch when the drop fell as near it. They had long since pulled away the ropy, carmine clots and threads that trailed in the water from the lowest splintered holes, shaking their ugly, sucker-topped heads and their elongated, tapering, thin-tailed bodies as they pulled. They were reluctant now to leave a place where they had fed so well and unexpectedly.

Inside the cockpit of the launch there were three other men. One, dead, lay on his back where he had fallen below the steering stool. Another, dead, lay humped big against the scupper by the starboard aft stanchion. The third, still alive, but long out of his head, lay on his side with his head on his arm.

The bilge of the launch was full of gasoline and when she rolled at all this made a sloshing sound. The man, Harry Morgan, believed this sound was in his own belly and it seemed to him now that his belly was big as a lake and that it sloshed on both shores at once. That was because he was on his back now with his knees drawn up and his head back. The water of the lake that was his belly was very cold; so cold that when he stepped into its edge it numbed him, and he was extremely cold now and everything tasted of gasoline as though he had been sucking on a hose to syphon a tank. He knew there was no tank although he could feel a cold rubber hose that seemed to have entered his mouth and now was coiled, big, cold, and heavy all down through him. Each time he took a breath the hose coiled colder and firmer in his lower abdomen and he could feel it like a big, smooth-moving snake in there, above the sloshing of the lake. He was afraid of it, but although it was in him, it

seemed a vast distance away and what he minded,
now, was the cold.

The cold was all through him, an aching cold that
would not numb away, and he lay quietly now and
felt it. For a time he had thought that if he could pull
himself up over himself it would warm him like a
blanket, and he thought for a while that he had gotten himself pulled up and he had started to warm.
But that warmth was really only the hemorrhage
produced by raising his knees up; and as the warmth
faded he knew now that you could not pull yourself
up over yourself and there was nothing to do about
the cold but take it. He lay there, trying hard in all of
him not to die long after he could not think. He was
in the shadow now, as the boat drifted, and it was
colder all the time.

The launch had been drifting since 10 o'clock of
the night before and it was now getting late in the afternoon. There was nothing else in sight across the
surface of the Gulf Stream but the gulf weed, a few
pink, inflated, membranous bubbles of Portuguese
men-of-war cocked jauntily on the surface, and the
distant smoke of a loaded tanker bound north from
Tampico.

CHAPTER TWENTY-ONE

"WELL," Richard Gordon said to his wife.

"You have lipstick on your shirt," she said. "And over your ear."

"What about this?"

"What about what?"

"What about finding you lying on the couch with that drunken slob?"

"You did not."

"Where did I find you?"

"You found us sitting on the couch."

"In the dark."

"Where have you been?"

"At the Bradleys'."

"Yes," she said. "I know. Don't come near me. You reek of that woman."

"What do you reek of?"

"Nothing. I've been sitting, talking to a friend."

"Did you kiss him?"

"No."

"Did he kiss you?"

"Yes, I liked it."

"You bitch."

"If you call me that I'll leave you."

"You bitch."

"All right," she said. "It's over. If you weren't so conceited and I weren't so good to you, you'd have seen it was over a long time ago."

"You bitch."

"No," she said. "I'm not a bitch. I've tried to be a good wife, but you're as selfish and conceited as a barnyard rooster. Always crowing, 'Look what I've done. Look how I've made you happy. Now run along and cackle.' Well, you don't make me happy and I'm sick of you. I'm through cackling."

"You shouldn't cackle. You never produced anything to cackle about."

"Whose fault was that? Didn't I want children? But we never could afford them. But we could afford to go to the Cap d'Antibes to swim and to Switzerland to ski. We can afford to come down here to Key West. I'm sick of you. I dislike you. This Bradley woman today was the last straw."

"Oh, leave her out of it."

"You coming home with lipstick all over you. Couldn't you even wash? There's some on your forehead, too."

"You kissed that drunken twirp."

"No, I didn't. But I would have if I'd known what you were doing."

"Why did you let him kiss you?"

"I was furious at you. We waited and waited and waited. You never came near me. You went off with that woman and stayed for hours. John brought me home."

"Oh, John, is it?"

"Yes, John. JOHN. John."

"And what's his last name? Thomas?"

"His name is MacWalsey."

"Why don't you spell it?"

"I can't," she said, and laughed. But it was the last time she laughed. "Don't think it's all right because I laugh," she said, tears in her eyes, her lips working. "It's not all right. This isn't just an ordinary row. It's over. I don't hate you. It isn't violent. I just dislike you. I dislike you thoroughly and I'm through with you."

"All right," he said.

"No. Not all right. All over. Don't you understand?"

"I guess so."

"Don't guess."

"Don't be so melodramatic, Helen."

"So I'm melodramatic, am I? Well, I'm not. I'm through with you."

"No, you're not."

"I won't say it again."

"What are you going to do?"

"I don't know yet. I may marry John MacWalsey."

"You will not."

"I will if I wish."

"He wouldn't marry you."

"Oh, yes, he will. He asked me to marry him this afternoon."

Richard Gordon said nothing. A hollow had come in him where his heart had been, and everything he heard, or said, seemed to be overheard.

"He asked you what?" he said, his voice coming from a long way away.

"To marry him."

"Why?"

"Because he loves me. Because he wants me to live with him. He makes enough money to support me."

"You're married to me."

"Not really. Not in the church. You wouldn't marry me in the church and it broke my poor mother's heart as you well know. I was so sentimental about you I'd break any one's heart for you. My, I was a damned fool. I broke my own heart, too. It's broken and gone. Everything I believed in and everything I cared about I left for you because you were so wonderful and you loved me so much that love was all that mattered. Love was the greatest thing, wasn't it? Love was what we had that no one else had or could ever have. And you were a genius and I was your whole life. I was your partner and your little black flower. Slop. Love is just another dirty lie. Love is ergoapiol pills to make me come around because you were afraid to have a baby. Love is quinine and quinine and quinine until I'm deaf with it. Love is that dirty aborting horror that you took me to. Love is my insides all messed up. It's half catheters and half whirling douches. I know about love. Love always hangs up behind the bathroom door. It smells like Lysol. To hell with love. Love is you making me happy and then going off to sleep with your mouth open while I lie awake all night afraid to say my prayers even because I know I have no right to any more. Love is all the dirty little tricks you taught me that you probably got out of some book. All right. I'm through with you and I'm through with love. Your kind of picknose love. You writer."

"You little mick slut."

"Don't call me names. I know the word for you."

"All right."

"No, not all right. All wrong and wrong again. If you were just a good writer I could stand for all the rest of it maybe. But I've seen you bitter, jealous, changing your politics to suit the fashion, sucking up to people's faces and talking about them behind their backs. I've seen you until I'm sick of you. Then that dirty rich bitch of a Bradley woman today. Oh, I'm sick of it. I've tried to take care of you and humor you and look after you and cook for you and keep quiet when you wanted and cheerful when you wanted and give you your little explosions and pretend it made me happy, and put up with your rages and jealousies and your meannesses and now I'm through."

"So now you want to start again with a drunken professor?"

"He's a man. He's kind and he's charitable and he makes you feel comfortable and we come from the same thing and we have values that you'll never have. He's like my father was."

"He's a drunk."

"He drinks. But so did my father. And my father wore wool socks and put his feet in them up on a chair and read the paper in the evening. And when we had croup he took care of us. He was a boiler maker and his hands were all broken and he liked to fight when he drank, and he could fight when he was sober. He went to mass because my mother wanted him to and he did his Easter duty for her and for Our Lord, but mostly for her, and he was a good union man and if he ever went with another woman she never knew it."

"I'll bet he went with plenty."

"Maybe he did, but if he did he told the priest, not her, and if he did it was because he couldn't help it and he was sorry and repented of it. He didn't do it out of curiosity, or from barnyard pride, or to tell his wife what a great man he was. If he did it was because my mother was away with us kids for the summer, and he was out with the boys and got drunk. He was a man."

"You ought to be a writer and write about him."

"I'd be a better writer than you. And John Mac-
Walsey is a good man. That's what you're not. You
couldn't be. No matter what your politics or your religion."

"I haven't any religion."

"Neither have I. But I had one once and I'm going to have one again. And you won't be there to
take it away. Like you've taken away everything
else."

"No."

"No. You can be in bed with some rich woman
like Helène Bradley. How did she like you? Did she
think you were wonderful?"

Looking at her sad, angry face, pretty with crying,
the lips swollen freshly like something after rain, her
curly dark hair wild about her face, Richard Gordon
gave her up, then, finally:

"And you don't love me any more?"

"I hate the word even."

"All right," he said, and slapped her hard and suddenly across the face.

She cried now from actual pain, not anger, her face
down on the table.

"You didn't need to do that," she said.

"Oh, yes, I did," he said. "You know an awful
lot, but you don't know how much I needed to do
that."

*That afternoon she had not seen him as the door
opened. She had not seen anything but the white*

ceiling with its cake-frosting modeling of cupids, doves and scroll work that the light from the open door suddenly made clear.

Richard Gordon had turned his head and seen him, standing heavy and bearded in the doorway.

"Don't stop," Helène had said. "Please don't stop." Her bright hair was spread over the pillow.

But Richard Gordon had stopped and his head was still turned, staring.

"Don't mind him. Don't mind anything. Don't you see you can't stop now?" the woman had said in desperate urgency.

The bearded man had closed the door softly. He was smiling.

"What's the matter, darling?" Helène Bradley had asked, now in the darkness again.

"I must go."

"Don't you see you can't go?"

"That man——"

"That's only Tommy," Helène had said. "He knows all about these things. Don't mind him. Come on, darling. Please do."

"I can't."

"You must," Helène had said. He could feel her shaking, and her head on his shoulder was trembling. "My God, don't you know anything? Haven't you any regard for a woman?"

"I have to go," said Richard Gordon.

In the darkness he had felt the slap across his face

that lighted flashes of light in his eyeballs. Then there was another slap. Across his mouth this time.

"So that's the kind of man you are," she had said to him. "I thought you were a man of the world. Get out of here."

That was this afternoon. That was how it had finished at the Bradleys'.

Now his wife sat with her head forward on her hands that rested on the table and neither of them said anything. Richard Gordon could hear the clock ticking and he felt as hollow as the room was quiet. After a while his wife said without looking at him: "I'm sorry it happened. But you see it's over, don't you?"

"Yes, if that's the way it's been."

"It hasn't been all like that, but for a long time it's been that way."

"I'm sorry I slapped you."

"Oh, that's nothing. That hasn't anything to do with it. That was just a way to say good-by."

"Don't."

"I'll have to get out," she said very tiredly. "I'll have to take the big suitcase, I'm afraid."

"Do it in the morning," he said. "You can do everything in the morning."

"I'd rather do it now, Dick, and it would be easier. But I'm so tired. It's made me awfully tired and given me a headache."

"You do whatever you want."

"Oh, God," she said. "I wish it wouldn't have happened. But it's happened. I'll try to fix everything up for you. You'll need somebody to look after you. If I hadn't of said some of that, or if you hadn't hit me, maybe we could have fixed it up again."

"No, it was over before that."

"I'm so sorry for you, Dick."

"Don't you be sorry for me or I'll slap you again."

"I guess I'd feel better if you slapped me," she said. "I *am* sorry for you. Oh, I *am*."

"Go to hell."

"I'm sorry I said it about you not being good in bed. I don't know anything about that. I guess you're wonderful."

"You're not such a star," he said.

She began to cry again.

"That's worse than slapping," she said.

"Well, what did you say?"

"I don't know. I don't remember. I was so angry and you hurt me so."

"Well, it's all over, so why be bitter?"

"Oh, I don't want it to be over. But it is and there's nothing to do now."

"You'll have your rummy professor."

"Don't," she said. "Can't we just shut up and not talk any more?"

"Yes."

"Will you?"

"Yes."

"I'll sleep out here."

"No. You can have the bed. You must. I'm going out for a while."

"Oh, don't go out."

"I've got to," he said.

"Good-by," she said, and he saw her face he always loved so much, that crying never spoiled, and her curly black hair, her small firm breasts under the sweater forward against the edge of the table, and he didn't see the rest of her that he'd loved so much and thought he had pleased, but evidently hadn't been any good to, that was all below the table, and as he went out the door she was looking at him across the table; and her chin was on her hands; and she was crying.

CHAPTER TWENTY-TWO

HE DID NOT take the bicycle but walked down the street. The moon was up now and the trees were dark against it, and he passed the frame houses with their narrow yards, light coming from the shuttered windows; the unpaved alleys, with their double rows of houses; Conch town, where all was starched, well-shuttered, virtue, failure, grits and boiled grunts, under-nourishment, prejudice, righteousness, inter-breeding and the comforts of religion; the open-doored, lighted Cuban bolito houses, shacks whose only romance was their names; The Red House, Chicha's; the pressed stone church; its steeples sharp, ugly triangles against the moonlight; the big grounds and the long, black-domed bulk of the convent, handsome in the moonlight; a filling station and a sandwich place, bright-lighted beside a vacant lot where a miniature golf course had been taken out; past the brightly lit main street with the three drug stores, the music store, the five Jew stores, three pool-rooms, two barbershops, five beer joints, three ice cream parlors, the five poor and the one good restaurant, two magazine and paper places, four second-hand joints (one of which made keys), a photographer's, an office building with four dentists' offices upstairs, the big dime store, a hotel on the corner with taxis opposite; and across, behind the hotel, to the street that led to jungle town, the big unpainted frame house with lights and the girls in the doorway, the mechanical piano going, and a sailor sitting in the street; and then on back, past the back of the brick courthouse with its clock luminous at half-past ten, past the whitewashed jail building shining in the moonlight, to the embowered entrance of the Lilac Time where motor cars filled the alley.

The Lilac Time was brightly lighted and full of people, and as Richard Gordon went in he saw the gambling room was crowded, the wheel turning and the little ball clicking brittle against metal partitions set in the bowl, the wheel turning slowly, the ball whirring, then clicking jumpily until it settled and there was only the turning of the wheel and the rattling of chips. At the bar, the proprietor who was serving with two bartenders, said "'Allo, 'allo, Mist' Gordon. What you have?"

"I don't know," said Richard Gordon.

"You don't look good. Whatsa matter? You don't feel good?"

"No."

"I fix you something just fine. Fix you up hokay. You ever try a Spanish absinthe, *ojen*?"

"Go ahead," said Gordon.

"You drink him you feel good. Want to fight anybody in a house," said the proprietor. "Make Mistah Gordon a *ojen* special."

Standing at the bar, Richard Gordon drank three *ojen* specials but he felt no better; the opaque, sweetish, cold, licorice-tasting drink did not make him feel any different.

"Give me something else," he said to the bartender.

"Whatsa matter? You no like a *ojen* special?" the proprietor asked. "You no feel good?"

"No."

"You got be careful what you drink after him."

"Give me a straight whiskey."

The whiskey warmed his tongue and the back of his throat, but it did not change his ideas any, and suddenly, looking at himself in the mirror behind the bar, he knew that drinking was never going to do any good to him now. Whatever he had now he had, and it was from now on, and if he drank himself unconscious when he woke up it would be there.

A tall, very thin young man with a sparse stubble of blonde beard on his chin who was standing next to him at the bar said, "Aren't you Richard Gordon?"

"Yes."

"I'm Herbert Spellman. We met at a party in Brooklyn one time I believe."

"Maybe," said Richard Gordon. "Why not?"

"I liked your last book very much," said Spellman. "I liked them all."

"I'm glad," said Richard Gordon. "Have a drink?"

"Have one with me," said Spellman. "Have you tried this *ojen*?"

"It's not doing me any good."

"What's the matter?"

"Feeling low."

"Wouldn't try another?"

"No. I'll have whiskey."

"You know, it's something to me to meet you," Spellman said. "I don't suppose you remember me at that party."

"No. But maybe it was a good party. You're not supposed to remember a good party, are you?"

"I guess not," said Spellman. "It was at Margaret Van Brunt's. Do you remember?" he asked hopefully.

"I'm trying to."

"I was the one set fire to the place," Spellman said.

"No," said Gordon.

"Yes," said Spellman, happily. "That was me. That was the greatest party I was ever on."

"What are you doing now?" Gordon asked.

"Not much," said Spellman. "I get around a little. I'm taking it sort of easy now. Are you writing a new book?"

"Yes. About half done."

"That's great," said Spellman. "What's it about?"

"A strike in a textile plant."

"That's marvellous," said Spellman. "You know I'm a sucker for anything on the social conflict."

"What?"

"I love it," said Spellman. "I go for it above anything else. You're absolutely the best of the lot. Listen, has it got a beautiful Jewish agitator in it?"

"Why?" asked Richard Gordon, suspiciously.

"It's a part for Sylvia Sidney. I'm in love with her. Want to see her picture?"

"I've seen it," said Richard Gordon.

"Let's have a drink," said Spellman, happily. "Think of meeting you down here. You know, I'm a lucky fellow. Really lucky."

"Why?" asked Richard Gordon.

"I'm crazy," said Spellman. "Gee, it's wonderful. It's just like being in love only it always comes out right."

Richard Gordon edged away a little.

"Don't be that way," said Spellman. "I'm not violent. That is, I'm almost never violent. Come on, let's have a drink."

"Have you been crazy long?"

"I think always," said Spellman. "I tell you it's the only way to be happy in times like these. What do I care what Douglas Aircraft does? What do I care what A. T. and T. does? They can't touch me. I just pick up one of your books or I take a drink, or I look at Sylvia's picture, and I'm happy. I'm like a bird. I'm better than a bird. I'm a—" he seemed to hesitate and hunt for a word, then hurried on. "I'm a lovely little stork," he blurted out and blushed. He looked at Richard Gordon fixedly, his lips working, and a large blonde young man detached himself from a group down the bar and coming toward him put a hand on his arm.

"Come on, Harold," he said. "We'd better be getting home."

Spellman looked at Richard Gordon wildly. "He sneered at a stork," he said. "He stepped away from a stork. A stork that wheels in circling flight—"

"Come on, Harold," said the big young man.

Spellman put out his hand to Richard Gordon. "No offence," he said. "You're a good writer. Keep right on with it. Remember I'm always happy. Don't let them confuse you. See you soon."

With the large young man's arm over his shoulder the two of them moved out through the crowd to the door. Spellman looked back and winked at Richard Gordon.

"Nice fella," the proprietor said. He tapped his head. "Very well educate. Studies too much I guess. Likes to break glasses. He don't mean no harm. Pay for everything he break."

"Does he come in here much?"

"In the evening. What he say he was? A swan?"

"A stork."

"Other night was a horse. With wings. Like a

horse on a white horse bottle only with pair a wings. Nice fella all right. Plenty money. Gets a funny ideas. Family keep him down here now with his manager. He told me he like your books, Mr. Gordon. What you have to drink? On the house."

"A whiskey," said Richard Gordon. He saw the sheriff coming toward him. The sheriff was an extremely tall, rather cadaverous and very friendly man. Richard Gordon had seen him that afternoon at the Bradleys' party and talked with him about the bank robbery.

"Say," said the sheriff, "if you're not doing anything come along with me a little later. The coast guard's towing in Harry Morgan's boat. A tanker signalled it up off Matacumbe. They've got the whole outfit."

"My God," said Richard Gordon. "They've got them all?"

"They're all dead except one man, the message said."

"You don't know who it is?"

"No, they didn't say. God knows what happened."

"Have they got the money?"

"Nobody knows. But it must be aboard if they didn't get to Cuba with it."

"When will they be in?"

"Oh, it will be two or three hours yet."

"Where will they bring the boat?"

"Into the Navy Yard, I suppose. Where the coast guard ties up."

"Where'll I see you to go down there?"

"I'll drop in here for you."

"Here or down at Freddy's. I can't stick it here much longer."

"It's pretty tough in at Freddy's tonight. It's full of those Vets from up on the Keys. They always raise the devil."

"I'll go down there and look at it," Richard Gordon said. "I'm feeling kind of low."

"Well, keep out of trouble," the sheriff said. "I'll pick you up there in a couple of hours. Want a lift down there?"

"Thanks."

They went out through the crowd and Richard Gordon got in beside the sheriff in his car.

"What do you suppose happened in Morgan's boat?" he asked.

"God knows," the sheriff said. "It sounds pretty grizzly."

"Didn't they have any other information?"

"Not a thing," said the sheriff. "Now look at that, will you?"

They were opposite the brightly lighted open front of Freddy's place and it was jammed to the sidewalk. Men in dungarees, some bareheaded, others in caps, old service hats and in cardboard helmets, crowded the bar three deep, and the loud-speaking nickle-in-the-slot phonograph was playing "Isle of Capri." As they pulled up a man came hurtling out of the open door, another man on top of him. They fell and rolled on the sidewalk, and the man on top, holding the other's hair in both hands, banged his head up and down on the cement, making a sickening noise. No one at the bar was paying any attention.

The sheriff got out of the car and grabbed the man on top by the shoulder.

"Cut it out," he said. "Get up there."

The man straightened up and looked at the sheriff. "For Christ sake, can't you mind your own business?"

The other man, blood in his hair, blood oozing from one ear, and more of it trickling down his freckled face, squared off at the sheriff.

"Leave my buddy alone," he said thickly. "What's the matter? Don't you think I can take it?"

"You can take it, Joey," the man who had been hammering him said. "Listen," to the sheriff, "could you let me take a buck?"

"No," said the sheriff.

"Go to hell then." He turned to Richard Gordon. "What about it, pal?"

"I'll buy you a drink," said Gordon.

"Come on," said the Vet, and took hold of Gordon's arm.

"I'll be by later," the sheriff said.

"Good. I'll be waiting for you."

As they edged in toward the end of the bar, the red-headed, freckle-faced man with the bloody ear and face gripped Gordon by the arm.

"My old buddy," he said.

"He's all right," the other Vet said. "He can take it."

"I can take it, see?" the bloody-faced one said. "That's where I got it on them."

"But you can't hand it out," some one said. "Cut out the shoving."

"Let us in," the bloody-faced one said. "Let in me and my old buddy." He whispered into Richard Gordon's ear, "I don't have to hand it out. I can take it, see?"

"Listen," the other Vet said as they finally reached the beer-wet bar, "you ought to have seen him at noon at the commissary at Camp Five. I had him down and I was hitting him on the head with a bottle. Just like playing on a drum. I bet I hit him fifty times."

"More," said the bloody-faced one.

"It didn't make no impression on him."

"I can take it," said the other. He whispered in Richard Gordon's ear, "It's a secret."

Richard Gordon handed over two of the three beers the white-jacketed, big-bellied nigger bartender drew and pushed toward him.

"What's a secret?" he asked.

"Me," said the bloody-faced one. "My secret."

"He's got a secret," the other Vet said. "He isn't lying."

"Want to hear it?" the bloody-faced one said in Richard Gordon's ear.

Gordon nodded.

"It don't hurt."

The other nodded. "Tell him the worst of it."

The red-headed one put his bloody lips almost to Gordon's ear.

"Sometimes it feels good," he said. "How do you feel about that?"

At Gordon's elbow was a tall, thin man with a scar that ran from one corner of his eye down over his chin. He looked down at the red-headed one and grinned.

"First it was an art," he said. "Then it became a pleasure. If things made me sick you'd make me sick, Red."

"You make sick easy," the first Vet said. "What outfit were you in?"

"It wouldn't mean anything to you, punch drunk," the tall man said.

"Have a drink?" Richard Gordon asked the tall man.

"Thanks," the other said. "I'm drinking."

"Don't forget us," said one of the two men Gordon had come in with.

"Three more beers," said Richard Gordon, and the Negro drew them and pushed them over. There was not elbow room to lift them in the crowd and Gordon was pressed against the tall man.

"You off a ship?" asked the tall man.

"No, staying here. You down from the Keys?"

"We came in tonight from Tortugas," the tall man said. "We raised enough hell so they couldn't keep us there."

"He's a red," the first Vet said.

"So would you be if you had any brains," the tall man said. "They sent a bunch of us there to get rid of us but we raised too much hell for them." He grinned at Richard Gordon.

"Nail that guy," somebody yelled, and Richard Gordon saw a fist hit a face that showed close to him. The man who was hit was pulled away from the bar by two others. In the clear, one man hit him again, hard, in the face, and the other hit him in the body. He went down on the cement floor and covered his head with his arms and one of the men kicked him in the small of the back. All this time he had not made a sound. One of the men jerked him to his feet and pushed him up against the wall.

"Cool the son-of-a-bitch," he said, and as the man sprawled, white faced against the wall, the second man set himself, knees slightly bent, and then swung up at him with a right fist that came from down near the cement floor and landed on the side of the white-faced man's jaw. He fell forward on his knees and then rolled slowly over, his head in a little pool of blood. The two men left him there and came back to the bar.

"Boy, you can hit," said one.

"That son-of-a-bitch comes in to town and puts all his pay in the postal savings and then hangs around here picking up drinks off the bar," the other said. "That's the second time I cooled him."

"You cooled him this time."

"When I hit him just then I felt his jaw go just like a bag of marbles," the other said happily. The man lay against the wall and nobody paid any attention to him.

"Listen, if you landed on me like that it wouldn't make no impression," the red-headed Vet said.

"Shut up, slappy," said the cooler. "You've got the old rale."

"No, I haven't."

"You punchies make me sick," the cooler said. "Why should I bust my hands on you?"

"That's just what you'd do, bust your hands," the red-headed one said. "Listen, pal," to Richard Gordon, "how's to have another?"

"Aren't they fine boys?" said the tall man. "War is a purifying and ennobling force. The question is whether only people like ourselves here are fitted to be soldiers or whether the different services have formed us."

"I don't know," said Richard Gordon.

"I would like to bet you that not three men in this room were drafted," the tall man said. "These are the elite. The very top cream of the scum. What

Wellington won at Waterloo with. Well, Mr. Hoover ran us out of Anticosti Flats and Mr. Roosevelt has shipped us down here to get rid of us. They've run the camp in a way to invite an epidemic, but the poor bastards won't die. They shipped a few of us to Tortugas but that's healthy now. Besides, we wouldn't stand for it. So they've brought us back. What's the next move? They've got to get rid of us. You can see that, can't you?"

"Why?"

"Because we are the desperate ones," the man said. "The ones with nothing to lose. We are the completely brutalized ones. We're worse than the stuff the original Spartacus worked with. But it's tough to try to do anything with because we have been beaten so far that the only solace is booze and the only pride is in being able to take it. But we're not all like that. There are some of us that are going to hand it out."

"Are there many Communists in the camp?"

"Only about forty," the tall man said. "Out of two thousand. It takes discipline and abnegation to be a Communist; a rummy can't be a Communist."

"Don't listen to him," the red-headed Vet said. "He's just a goddamn radical."

"Listen," the other Vet who was drinking beer with Richard Gordon said, "let me tell you about in the Navy. Let me tell you, you goddamn radical."

"Don't listen to him," the red-headed one said. "When the fleet's in New York and you go ashore

there in the evening up under Riverside Drive there's
old guys with long beards come down and you can
piss in their beards for a dollar. What do you think
about that?"

"I'll buy you a drink," said the tall man, "and you
forget that one. I don't like to hear that one."

"I don't forget anything," the red-headed one said.
"What's the matter with you, pal?"

"Is that true about the beards?" Richard Gordon
asked. He felt a little sick.

"I swear to God and my mother," the red-headed
one said. "Hell, that ain't nothing."

Up the bar a Vet was arguing with Freddy about
the payment of a drink.

"That's what you had," said Freddy.

Richard Gordon watched the Vet's face. He was
very drunk, his eyes were bloodshot and he was looking for trouble.

"You're a goddamn liar," he said to Freddy.

"Eighty-five cents," Freddy said to him.

"Watch this," said the red-headed Vet.

Freddy spread his hands on the bar. He was
watching the Vet.

"You're a goddamn liar," said the Vet, and picked
up a beer glass to throw it. As his hand closed on it,
Freddy's right hand swung in a half circle over the
bar and cracked a big saltcellar covered with a bar
towel alongside the Vet's head.

"Was it neat?" said the red-headed Vet. "Was it
pretty?"

"You ought to see him tap them with that sawed-off billiard cue," the other said.

Two Vets standing next to where the saltcellar man had slipped down looked at Freddy angrily. "What's the idea of cooling him?"

"Take it easy," said Freddy. "This one is on the house. Hey, Wallace," he said. "Put that fellow over against the wall."

"Was it pretty?" the red-headed Vet asked Richard Gordon. "Wasn't that sweet?"

A heavy-set young fellow had dragged the saltcellared man out through the crowd. He pulled him to his feet and the man looked at him vacantly. "Run along," he said to him. "Get yourself some air."

Over against the wall the man who had been cooled sat with his head in his hands. The heavy-set young man went over to him.

"You run along, too," he said to him. "You just get in trouble here."

"My jaw's broken," the cooled one said thickly. Blood was running out of his mouth and down over his chin.

"You're lucky you aren't killed, that wallop he hit you," the thick-set young man said. "You run along now."

"My jaw's broke," the other said dully. "They broke my jaw."

"You better run along," the young man said. "You just get in trouble here."

He helped the jaw-broken man to his feet and he staggered unsteadily out to the street.

"I've seen a dozen laying against the wall over there on a big night," the red-headed Vet said. "One morning I seen that big boogie there mopping it up with a bucket. Didn't I see you mop it up with a bucket?" he asked the big Negro bartender.

"Yes, sir," said the bartender. "Plenty of times. Yes, sir. But you never seen me fight nobody."

"Didn't I tell you?" said the red-headed Vet. "With a bucket."

"This looks like a big night coming on," the other Vet said. "What do you say, pal?" to Richard Gordon. "O.K. we have another one?"

Richard Gordon could feel himself getting drunk. His face, reflected in the mirror behind the bar, was beginning to look strange to him.

"What's your name?" he asked the tall Communist.

"Jacks," the tall man said. "Nelson Jacks."

"Where were you before you came here?"

"Oh, around," the man said. "Mexico, Cuba, South America, and around."

"I envy you," said Richard Gordon.

"Why envy me? Why don't you get to work?"

"I've written three books," Richard Gordon said. "I'm writing one now about Gastonia."

"Good," said the tall man. "That's fine. What did you say your name was?"

"Richard Gordon."

"Oh," said the tall man.

"What do you mean, 'oh'?"

"Nothing," said the tall man.

"Did you ever read the books?" Richard Gordon asked.

"Yes."

"Didn't you like them?"

"No," said the tall man.

"Why?"

"I don't like to say."

"Go ahead."

"I thought they were shit," the tall man said and turned away.

"I guess this is my night," said Richard Gordon. "This is my big night. What did you say you'd have?" he asked the red-headed Vet. "I've got two dollars left."

"One beer," said the red-headed man. "Listen, you're my pal. I think your books are fine. To hell with that radical bastard."

"You haven't got a book with you?" asked the other Vet. "Pal, I'd like to read one. Did you ever write for *Western Stories,* or *War Aces?* I could read that *War Aces* every day."

"Who is that tall bird?" asked Richard Gordon.

"I tell you he's just a radical bastard," said the second Vet. "The camp's full of them. We'd run them out, but I tell you half the time most of the guys in camp can't remember."

"Can't remember what?" asked the red-headed one.

"Can't remember anything," said the other.

"You see me?" asked the red-headed one.

"Yes," said Richard Gordon.

"Would you guess I got the finest little wife in the world?"

"Why not?"

"Well, I have," said the red-headed one. "And that girl is nuts about me. She's like a slave. 'Give me another cup of coffee,' I say to her. 'O.K., Pop,' she says. And I get it. Anything else the same way. She's carried away with me. If I got a whim, it's her law."

"Only where is she?" asked the other Vet.

"That's it," said the red-headed one. "That's it, pal. Where is she?"

"He don't know where she is," the second Vet said.

"Not only that," said the red-headed one. "I don't know where I saw her last."

"He don't even know what country she's in."

"But listen, buddy," said the red-headed one. "Wherever she is, that little girl is faithful."

"That's God's truth," said the other Vet. "You can stake your life on that."

"Sometimes," said the red-headed one, "I think that she is maybe Ginger Rogers and that she has gone into the moving pictures."

"Why not?" said the other.

"Then again, I just see her waiting there quietly where I live."

"Keeping the home fires burning," said the other.

"That's it," said the red-headed one. "She's the finest little woman in the world."

"Listen," said the other, "my old mother is O.K., too."

"That's right."

"She's dead," said the second Vet. "Let's not talk about her."

"Aren't you married, pal?" the red-headed Vet asked Richard Gordon.

"Sure," he said. Down the bar, about four men away, he could see the red face, the blue eyes and sandy, beer-dewed mustache of Professor MacWalsey. Professor MacWalsey was looking straight ahead of him and as Richard Gordon watched he finished his glass of beer and, raising his lower lip, removed the foam from his mustache. Richard Gordon noticed how bright blue his eyes were.

As Richard Gordon watched him he felt a sick feeling in his chest. And he knew for the first time how a man feels when he looks at the man his wife is leaving him for.

"What's the matter, pal?" asked the red-headed Vet.

"Nothing."

"You don't feel good. I can tell you feel bad."

"No," said Richard Gordon.

"You look like you seen a ghost."

"You see that fellow down there with a mustache?" asked Richard Gordon.

"Him?"

"Yes."

"What about him?" asked the second Vet.

"Nothing," said Richard Gordon. "Goddamn it. Nothing."

"Is he a bother to you? We can cool him. The three of us can jump him and you can put the boots to him."

"No," said Richard Gordon. "It wouldn't do any good."

"We'll get him when he goes outside," the red-headed Vet said. "I don't like the look of him. The son-of-a-bitch looks like a scab to me."

"I hate him," said Richard Gordon. "He's ruined my life."

"We'll give him the works," said the second Vet. "The yellow rat. Listen Red, get a hold of a couple of bottles. We'll beat him to death. Listen, when did he do it, pal? O.K. we have another one?"

"We've got a dollar and seventy cents," Richard Gordon said.

"Maybe we better get a pint then," the red-headed Vet said. "My teeth are floating now."

"No," said the other. "This beer is good for you. This is draft beer. Stick with the beer. Let's go and beat this guy up and come back drink some more beer."

"No. Leave him alone."

"No, pal. Not us. You said that rat ruined your wife."

"My life. Not my wife."

"Jese! Pardon me. I'm sorry, pal."

"He defaulted and ruined the bank," the other Vet said. "I'll bet there's a reward for him. By God, I seen a picture of him at the post office today."

"What were you doing at the post office?" asked the other suspiciously.

"Can't I get a letter?"

"What's the matter with getting letters at camp?"

"Do you think I went to the postal savings?"

"What were you doing in the post office?"

"I just stopped by."

"Take that," said his pal and swung on him as well as he could in the crowd.

"There goes those two cell mates," said somebody. Holding and punching, kneeing and butting, the two were pushed out of the door.

"Let 'em fight on the sidewalk," the wide-shouldered young man said. "Those bastards fight three or four times a night."

"They're a couple of punchies," another Vet said. "Red could fight once but he's got the old rale."

"They've both got it."

"Red got it fighting a fellow in the ring," a short chunky Vet said. "This fellow had the old rale and he was all broke out on the shoulders and back. Every time they'd go into a clinch he'd rub his shoulder under Red's nose or across his puss."

"Oh, nuts. What did he put his face there for?"

"That was the way Red carried his head when he was in close. Down, like this. And this fellow was just roughing him."

"Oh, nuts. That story is all bull. Nobody ever got the old rale from anybody in a fight."

"That's what you think. Listen, Red was as clean a living kid as you ever saw. I knew him. He was in my outfit. He was a good little fighter, too. I mean good. He was married, too, to a nice girl. I mean nice. And this Benny Sampson gave him that old rale just as sure as I'm standing here."

"Then sit down," said another Vet. "How did Poochy get it?"

"He got it in Shanghai."

"Where did you get yours?"

"I ain't got it."

"Where did Suds get it?"

"Off a girl in Brest, coming home."

"That's all you guys ever talk about. The old rale. What difference does the old rale make?"

"None, the way we are now," one Vet said. "You're just as happy with it."

"Poochy's happier. He don't know where he is."

"What's the old rale?" Professor MacWalsey asked the man next to him at the bar. The man told him.

"I wonder what the derivation is," Professor MacWalsey said.

"I don't know," said the man. "I've always heard it called the old rale since my first enlistment. Some call it ral. But usually they call it the old rale."

"I'd like to know," said Professor MacWalsey. "Most of those terms are old English words."

"Why do they call it the old rale?" the Vet next to Professor MacWalsey asked another.

"I don't know."

Nobody seemed to know but all enjoyed the atmosphere of serious philological discussion.

Richard Gordon was next to Professor MacWalsey at the bar now. When Red and Poochy had started fighting he had been pushed down there and he had not resisted the move.

"Hello," Professor MacWalsey said to him. "Do you want a drink?"

"Not with you," said Richard Gordon.

"I suppose you're right," said Professor MacWalsey. "Did you ever see anything like this?"

"No," said Richard Gordon.

"It's very strange," said Professor MacWalsey.

"They're amazing. I always come here nights."

"Don't you ever get in trouble?"

"No. Why should I?"

"Drunken fights."

"I never seem to have any trouble."

"A couple of friends of mine wanted to beat you up a couple of minutes ago."

"Yes."

"I wish I would have let them."

"I don't think it would make much difference," said Professor MacWalsey in the odd way of speaking he had. "If I annoy you by being here I can go."

"No," said Richard Gordon. "I sort of like to be near you."

"Yes," said Professor MacWalsey.

"Have you ever been married?" asked Richard Gordon.

"Yes."

"What happened?"

"My wife died during the influenza epidemic in 1918."

"Why do you want to marry again now?"

"I think I'd be better at it now. I think perhaps I'd be a better husband now."

"So you picked my wife."

"Yes," said Professor MacWalsey.

"Damn you," said Richard Gordon, and hit him in the face.

Some one grabbed his arm. He jerked it loose and some one hit him crashingly behind the ear. He could see Professor MacWalsey, before him, still at the bar, his face red, blinking his eyes. He was reaching for another beer to replace the one Gordon had spilled, and Richard Gordon drew back his arm to hit him again. As he did so, something exploded again behind his ear and all the lights flared up, wheeled round, and then went out.

Then he was standing in the doorway of Freddy's place. His head was ringing, and the crowded room was unsteady and wheeling slightly, and he felt sick to his stomach. He could see the crowd looking at him. The big-shouldered young man was standing by him. "Listen," he was saying, "you don't want to start any trouble in here. There's enough fights in here with those rummies."

"Who hit me?" asked Richard Gordon.

"I hit you," said the wide young man. "That fellow's a regular customer here. You want to take it easy. You don't want to go to fight in here."

Standing unsteadily Richard Gordon saw Professor MacWalsey coming toward him away from the crowd at the bar. "I'm sorry," he said. "I didn't want anybody to slug you. I don't blame you for feeling the way you do."

"Goddamn you," said Richard Gordon, and started toward him. It was the last thing he remembered doing for the wide young man set himself, dropped his shoulders slightly, and clipped him again, and he went down, this time, on the cement floor on his face. The wide young man turned to Professor MacWalsey. "That's all right, Doc," he said, hospitably. "He won't annoy you now. What's the matter with him anyway?"

"I've got to take him home," said Professor Mac-Walsey. "Will he be all right?"

"Sure."

"Help me to get him in a taxi," said Professor MacWalsey. They carried Richard Gordon out between them and with the driver helping, put him in the old Model T taxi.

"You're sure he'll be all right?" asked Professor MacWalsey.

"Just pull on his ears good when you want to bring him to. Put some water on him. Look out he don't want to fight when he comes to. Don't let him grab you, Doc."

"No," said Professor MacWalsey.

Richard Gordon's head lay back at an odd angle in the back of the taxi and he made a heavy, rasping noise when he breathed. Professor MacWalsey put his arm under his head and held it so it did not bump against the seat.

"Where are we going?" asked the taxi driver.

"Out on the other end of town," said Professor MacWalsey. "Past the Park. Down the street from the place where they sell mullets."

"That's the Rocky Road," the driver said.

"Yes," said Professor MacWalsey.

As they passed the first coffee shop up the street, Professor MacWalsey told the driver to stop. He wanted to go in and get some cigarettes. He laid Richard Gordon's head down carefully on the seat and went into the coffee shop. When he came out to get back into the taxi, Richard Gordon was gone.

"Where did he go?" he asked the driver.

"That's him up the street," the driver said.

"Catch up with him."

As the taxi pulled up even with him, Professor MacWalsey got out and went up to Richard Gordon who was lurching along the sidewalk.

"Come on, Gordon," he said. "We're going home."

Richard Gordon looked at him.

"We?" he said, swaying.

"I want you to go home in this taxi."

"You go to hell."

"I wish you'd come," Professor MacWalsey said. "I want you to get home safely."

"Where's your gang?" said Richard Gordon.

"What gang?"

"Your gang that beat me up."

"That was the bouncer. I didn't know he was going to hit you."

"You lie," said Richard Gordon. He swung at the red-faced man in front of him and missed him. He slipped forward onto his knees and got up slowly.

His knees were scraped raw from the sidewalk, but he did not know it.

"Come on and fight," he said brokenly.

"I don't fight," said Professor MacWalsey. "If you'll get into the taxi I'll leave you."

"Go to hell," said Richard Gordon and started down the street.

"Leave him go," said the taxi driver. "He's all right now."

"Do you think he'll be all right?"

"Hell," the taxi driver said. "He's perfect."

"I'm worried about him," Professor MacWalsey said.

"You can't get him in without fighting him," the taxi driver said. "Let him go. He's fine. Is he your brother?"

"In a way," said Professor MacWalsey.

He watched Richard Gordon lurching down the street until he was out of sight in the shadow from the big trees whose branches dipped down to grow into the ground like roots. What he was thinking as he watched him was not pleasant. It is a mortal sin, he thought, a grave and deadly sin and a great cruelty, and while technically one's religion may permit the ultimate result, I cannot pardon myself. On the other hand, a surgeon cannot desist while operating for fear of hurting the patient. But why must all the operations in life be performed without an anaesthetic? If I had been a better man I would have let him beat me up. It would have been better for him. The poor stupid man. The poor homeless man. I ought to stay with him, but I know that is too much for him to bear. I am ashamed and disgusted with myself and I hate what I have done. It all may turn out badly too. But I must not think about that. I will now return to the anaesthetic I have used for seventeen years and will not need much longer. Although it is probably a vice now for which I only invent excuses. Though at least it is a vice for which I am suited. But I wish I could help that poor man whom I am wronging.

"Drive me back to Freddy's," he said.

CHAPTER TWENTY-THREE

THE COAST GUARD cutter towing the *Queen Conch* was coming down the hawk channel between the reef and the Keys. The cutter rolled in the cross chop the light north wind raised against the flood tide but the white boat was towing easily and well.

"She'll be all right if it doesn't breeze," the coast guard captain said. "She tows pretty, too. That Robby built nice boats. Could you make out any of the guff he was talking?"

"He didn't make any sense," the mate said. "He's way out of his head."

"I guess he'll die all right," the captain said. "Shot in the belly that way. Do you suppose he killed those four Cubans?"

"You can't tell. I asked him but he didn't know what I was saying."

"Should we go talk to him again?"

"Let's have a look at him," the captain said.

Leaving the quartermaster at the wheel, running the beacons down the channel, they went behind the wheelhouse into the captain's cabin. Harry Morgan lay there on the iron pipe bunk. His eyes were closed but he opened them when the captain touched his wide shoulder.

"How you feeling, Harry?" the captain asked him. Harry looked at him and did not speak.

"Can we get you anything, boy?" the captain asked him.

Harry Morgan looked at him.

"He don't hear you," said the mate.

"Harry," said the captain, "do you want anything, boy?"

He wet a towel in the water bottle on a gimbal by the bunk and moistened Harry Morgan's deeply cracked lips. They were dry and black looking. Looking at him, Harry Morgan started speaking. "A man," he said.

"Sure," said the captain. "Go on."

"A man," said Harry Morgan, very slowly. "Ain't got no hasn't got any can't really isn't any way out." He stopped. There had been no expression on his face at all when he spoke.

"Go on, Harry," said the captain. "Tell us who did it. How did it happen, boy?"

"A man," said Harry, looking at him now with his narrow eyes on the wide, high-cheek-boned face, trying now to tell him.

"Four men," said the captain helpfully. He moistened the lips again, squeezing the towel so a few drops went between them.

"A man," corrected Harry; then stopped.

"All right. A man," the captain said.

"A man," Harry said again very flatly, very slowly,

talking with his dry mouth. "Now the way things are the way they go no matter what no."

The captain looked at the mate and shook his head.

"Who did it, Harry?" the mate asked.

Harry looked at him.

"Don't fool yourself," he said. The captain and the mate both bent over him. Now it was coming. "Like trying to pass cars on the top of hills. On that road in Cuba. On any road. Anywhere. Just like that. I mean how things are. The way that they been going. For a while yes sure all right. Maybe with luck. A man." He stopped. The captain shook his head at the mate again. Harry Morgan looked at him flatly. The captain wet Harry's lips again. They made a bloody mark on the towel.

"A man," Harry Morgan said, looking at them both. "One man alone ain't got. No man alone now." He stopped. "No matter how a man alone ain't got no bloody fucking chance."

He shut his eyes. It had taken him a long time to get it out and it had taken him all of his life to learn it.

He lay there his eyes open again.

"Come on," said the captain to the mate. "You sure you don't want anything, Harry?"

Harry Morgan looked at him but he did not answer. He had told them, but they had not heard.

"We'll be back," said the captain. "Take it easy, boy."

Harry Morgan watched them go out of the cabin.

Forward in the wheelhouse, watching it get dark and the light of Sombrero starting to sweep out at sea, the mate said, "He gives you the willies out of his head like that."

"Poor fellow," said the captain. "Well, we'll be in pretty soon now. We'll get him in soon after midnight. If we don't have to slow down for that tow."

"Think he'll live?"

"No," said the captain. "But you can't ever tell."

CHAPTER TWENTY-FOUR

THERE WERE many people in the dark street outside the iron gates that closed the entrance to the old
submarine base now transformed into a yacht basin.
The Cuban watchman had orders to let no one in,
and the crowd were pressing against the fence to look
through between the iron rods into the dark enclo-
sure lit, along the water, by the lights of the yachts
that lay moored at the finger piers. The crowd was as
quiet as only a Key West crowd can be. The yachtsmen pushed and elbowed their way through to the
gate and by the watchman.

"Hey. You canna comein," the watchman said.

"What the hell. We're off a yacht."

"Nobody supposacomein," the watchman said.
"Get back."

"Don't be stupid," said one of the yachtsmen, and
pushed him aside to go up the road toward the dock.

Behind them was the crowd outside the gates,
where the little watchman stood uncomfortable and
anxious in his cap, his long mustache and his di-
shevelled authority, wishing he had a key to lock the
big gate and, as they strode heartily up the sloping
road they saw ahead, then passed, a group of men

waiting at the Coast Guard pier. They paid no attention to them but walked along the dock, past the piers where the other yachts lay to pier number five, and out on the pier to where the gang plank reached, in the glare of a flood light, from rough wooden pier to the teak deck of the *New Exuma II*. In the main cabin they sat in big leather chairs beside a long table on which magazines were spread, and one of them rang for the steward.

"Scotch and soda," he said. "You, Henry?"

"Yes," said Henry Carpenter.

"What was the matter with that silly ass at the gate?"

"I've no idea," said Henry Carpenter.

The steward, in his white jacket, brought the two glasses.

"Play those disks I put out after dinner," the yachtsman, whose name was Wallace Johnston, said.

"I'm afraid I put them away, sir," the steward said.

"Damn you," said Wallace Johnston. "Play that new Bach album then."

"Very good, sir," said the steward. He went over to the record cabinet and took out an album and moved with it to the phonograph. He began playing the "Sarabande."

"Did you see Tommy Bradley today?" asked Henry Carpenter. "I saw him as the plane came in."

"I can't bear him," said Wallace. "Neither him nor that whore of a wife of his."

"I like Helène," said Henry Carpenter. "She has such a good time."

"Did you ever try it?"

"Of course. It's marvellous."

"I can't stick her at any price," said Wallace Johnston. "Why in God's name does she live down here?"

"They have a lovely place."

"It is a nice clean little yacht basin," said Wallace Johnston. "Is it true Tommy Bradley's impotent?"

"I shouldn't think so. You hear that about every one. He's simply broad minded."

"Broad minded is excellent. She's certainly a broad if there ever was one."

"She's a remarkably nice woman," said Henry Carpenter. "You'd like her, Wally."

"I would not," said Wallace. "She represents everything I hate in a woman, and Tommy Bradley epitomizes everything I hate in a man."

"You feel awfully strongly tonight."

"You never feel strongly because you have no consistency," Wallace Johnston said. "You can't make up your mind. You don't know what you are even."

"Let's drop me," said Henry Carpenter. He lit a cigarette.

"Why should I?"

"Well, one reason you might is because I go with you on your bloody yacht, and at least half the time I do what you want to do, and that keeps you from paying blackmail to the bus boys and sailors, and one thing and another, that do know what they are, and what you are."

"You're in a pretty mood," said Wallace Johnston. "You know I never pay blackmail."

"No. You're too tight to. You have friends like me instead."

"I haven't any other friends like you."

"Don't be charming," said Henry. "I don't feel up to it tonight. Just go ahead and play Bach and abuse your steward and drink a little too much and go to bed."

"What's gotten into you?" said the other, standing up. "Why are you getting so damned unpleasant? You're not such a great bargain, you know."

"I know," said Henry. "I'll be oh so jolly tomorrow. But tonight's a bad night. Didn't you ever notice any difference in nights? I suppose when you're rich enough there isn't any difference."

"You talk like a school girl."

"Good night," said Henry Carpenter. "I'm not a school girl nor a school boy. I'm going to bed. Everything will be awfully jolly in the morning."

"What did you lose? Is that what makes you so gloomy?"

"I lost three hundred."

"See? I told you that was it."

"You always know, don't you?"

"But look. You lost three hundred."

"I've lost more than that."

"How much more?"

"The jackpot," said Henry Carpenter. "The eternal jackpot. I'm playing a machine now that doesn't give jackpots any more. Only tonight I just happened to think about it. Usually I don't think about it. Now I'm going to bed so I won't bore you."

"You don't bore me. But just try not to be rude."

"I'm afraid I'm rude and you bore me. Good night. Everything will be fine tomorrow."

"You're damned rude."

"Take it or leave it," said Henry. "I've been doing both all my life."

"Good night," said Wallace Johnston hopefully.

Henry Carpenter did not answer. He was listening to the Bach.

"Don't go off to bed like that," Wallace Johnston said. "Why be so temperamental?"

"Drop it."

"Why should I? I've seen you come out of it before."

"Drop it."

"Have a drink and cheer up."

"I don't want a drink and it wouldn't cheer me up."

"Well, go off to bed, then."

"I am," said Henry Carpenter.

That was how it was that night on the *New Exuma II*, with a crew of twelve, Captain Nils Larson, master, and on board Wallace Johnston, owner, 38

years old, M.A. Harvard, composer, money from
silk mills, unmarried, *interdit de sejour* in Paris,
well known from Algiers to Biskra, and one guest,
Henry Carpenter, 36, M.A. Harvard, money now
two hundred a month in trust fund from his mother,
formerly four hundred and fifty a month until the
bank administering the Trust Fund had exchanged
one good security for another good security, for other
not so good securities, and, finally, for an equity in
an office building the bank had been saddled with
and which paid nothing at all. Long before this re-
duction in income it had been said of Henry Carpenter that if he were dropped from a height of 5500
feet without a parachute, he would land safely with
his knees under some rich man's table. But he gave
value in good company for his entertainment and
while it was only lately, and rarely, that he felt, or
expressed himself, as he had tonight, his friends had
felt for some time that he was cracking up. If he
had not been felt to be cracking up, with that instinct
for feeling something wrong with a member of the
pack and healthy desire to turn him out, if it is impossible to destroy him, which characterizes the rich,
he would not have been reduced to accepting the hos-
pitality of Wallace Johnston. As it was, Wallace
Johnston, with his rather special pleasures, was
Henry Carpenter's last stand, and he was defending
his position better than he knew for his honest court-
ing of an end to their relationship; his subsequent

brutality of expression, and sincere insecurity of tenure intrigued and seduced the other who might, given Henry Carpenter's age, have easily been bored by a steady compliance. Thus Henry Carpenter postponed his inevitable suicide by a matter of weeks if not of months.

The money on which it was not worth while for him to live was one hundred and seventy dollars more a month than the fisherman Albert Tracy had been supporting his family on at the time of his death three days before.

Aboard the other yachts lying at the finger piers there were other people with other problems. On one of the largest yachts, a handsome, black, barkentine rigged three-master, a sixty-year-old grain broker lay awake worrying about the report he had received from his office of the activities of the investigators from the Internal Revenue Bureau. Ordinarily, at this time of night, he would have quieted his worry with Scotch high balls and have reached the state where he felt as tough and regardless of consequences as any of the old brothers of the coast with whom, in character and standards of conduct, he had, truly, much in common. But his doctor had forbidden him all liquor for a month, for three months really, that is they had said it would kill him in a year if he did not give up alcohol for at least three months, so he was going to lay off it for a month; and now he worried about the call he had

received from the Bureau before he left town asking
him exactly where he was going and whether he
planned to leave the United States coastal waters.

He lay, now, in his pyjamas, on his wide bed, two
pillows under his head, the reading light on, but he
could not keep his mind on the book, which was an
account of a trip to Galapagos. In the old days he had
never brought them to this bed. He'd had them in
their cabins and he came to this bed afterwards. This
was his own stateroom, as private to him as his office.
He never wanted a woman in his room. When he
wanted one he went to hers, and when he was
through he was through, and now that he was
through for good his brain had the same clear cold-
ness always that had, in the old days, been an after effect. And he lay now, with no kindly blurring, denied
all that chemical courage that had soothed his mind
and warmed his heart for so many years, and won-
dered what the department had, what they had
found and what they would twist, what they would
accept as normal and what they would insist was eva-
sion; and he was not afraid of them, but only hated
them and the power they would use so insolently that
all his own hard, small, tough and lasting insolence,
the one permanent thing he had gained and that was
truly valid, would be drilled through, and, if he were
ever made afraid, shattered.

He did not think in any abstractions, but in deals,
in sales, in transfers and in gifts. He thought in

shares, in bales, in thousands of bushels, in options, holding companies, trusts, and subsidiary corpora- tions, and as he went over it he knew they had plenty, enough so he would have no peace for years. If they would not compromise it would be very bad. In the old days he would not have worried, but the fighting part of him was tired now, along with the other part, and he was alone in all of this now and he lay on the big, wide, old bed and could neither read nor sleep.

His wife had divorced him ten years before after twenty years of keeping up appearances, and he had never missed her nor had he ever loved her. He had started with her money and she had borne him two male children, both of whom, like their mother, were fools. He had treated her well until the money he had made was double her original capital and then he could afford to take no notice of her. After his money had reached that point he had never been annoyed by her sick headaches, by her complaints, or by her plans. He had ignored them.

He had been admirably endowed for a speculative career because he had possessed extraordinary sexual vitality which gave him the confidence to gamble well; common sense, an excellent mathematical brain, a permanent but controlled skepticism; a skepticism which was as sensitive to impending disaster as an ac- curate aneroid barometer to atmospheric pressure; and a valid time sense that kept him from trying to hit tops or bottoms. These, coupled with a lack of

morals, an ability to make people like him without
ever liking or trusting them in return, while at the
same time convincing them warmly and heartily of
his friendship; not a disinterested friendship, but a
friendship so interested in their success that it auto-
matically made them accomplices; and an incapacity
for either remorse or pity, had carried him to where
he was now. And where he was now was lying in a
pair of striped silk pyjamas that covered his shrunken
old man's chest, his bloated little belly, his now useless and disproportionately large equipment that had
once been his pride, and his small flabby legs, lying
on a bed unable to sleep because he finally had remorse.

His remorse was to think if only he had not been
quite so smart five years ago. He could have paid the
taxes then without any juggling, and if he had only
done so he would be all right now. So he lay thinking
of that and finally he slept; but because remorse had
once found the crack and begun to seep in, he did not
know he slept because his brain kept on as it had
while he was awake. So there would be no rest and,
at his age, it would not take so long for that to get
him.

He used to say that only suckers worried and he
would keep from worrying now until he could not
sleep. He might keep from it until he slept, but then
it would come in, and since he was this old its task
was easy.

He would not need to worry about what he had done to other people, nor what had happened to them due to him, nor how they'd ended; who'd moved from houses on the Lake Shore drive to taking boarders out in Austin, whose debutante daughters now were dentists' assistants when they had a job; who ended up a night watchman at sixty-three after that last corner; who shot himself early one morning before breakfast and which one of his children found him, and what the mess looked like; who now rode on the L to work, when there was work, from Berwyn, trying to sell, first, bonds; then motor cars; then house-to-housing novelties and specialties (we don't want no peddlers, get out of here, the door slammed in his face) until he varied the leaning drop his father made from forty-two floors up, with no rush of plumes as when an eagle falls, to a step forward onto the third rail in front of the Aurora-Elgin train, his overcoat pocket full of unsaleable combination eggbeaters and fruit juice extracters. *Just let me demonstrate it, madame. You attach it here, screw down on this little gadget here. Now watch.* No, I don't want it. *Just try one.* I don't want it. Get out.

So he got out onto the sidewalk with the framehouses, the naked yards and the bare catalpa trees where no one wanted it or anything else, that led down to the Aurora-Elgin tracks.

Some made the long drop from the apartment

or the office window; some took it quietly in two-car garages with the motor running; some used the native tradition of the Colt or Smith and Wesson; those well-constructed implements that end insomnia, terminate remorse, cure cancer, avoid bankruptcy, and blast an exit from intolerable positions by the pressure of a finger; those admirable American instruments so easily carried, so sure of effect, so well designed to end the American dream when it becomes a nightmare, their only drawback the mess they leave for relatives to clean up.

The men he broke made all these various exits but that never worried him. Somebody had to lose and only suckers worried.

No he would not have to think of them nor of the by-products of successful speculation. You win; somebody's got to lose, and only suckers worry.

It would be enough for him to think about how much it would be better if he had not been quite so smart five years ago, and in a little while, at his age, the wish to change what can no longer be undone, will open up the gap that will let worry in. Only suckers worry. But he can knock the worry if he takes a Scotch and soda. The hell with what the doctor said. So he rings for one and the steward comes sleepily, and as he drinks it, the speculator is not a sucker now; except for death.

While on the next yacht beyond, a pleasant, dull and upright family are asleep. The father's conscience is good and he sleeps soundly on his side, a clipper ship running before a blow framed above his head, the reading light on, a book dropped beside the bed. The mother sleeps well and dreams about her garden. She is fifty but is a handsome, wholesome, well-kept woman who looks attractive as she sleeps. The daughter dreams about her fiancé who comes tomorrow on the plane and she stirs in her sleep and laughs at something in the dream and, without waking, raises her knees almost against her chin, curled up like a cat, with curly blonde hair and her smooth-skinned pretty face, asleep she looks as her mother did when she was a girl.

They are a happy family and all love each other. The father is a man of civic pride and many good works, who opposed prohibition, is not bigoted and is generous, sympathetic, understanding and almost never irritable. The crew of the yacht are well-paid, well-fed and have good quarters. They all think highly of the owner and like his wife and daughter. The fiancé is a Skull and Bones man, voted most likely to succeed, voted most popular, who still thinks more of others than of himself and would be too good for any one except a lovely girl like Frances. He is probably a little too good for Frances too, but it will be years before Frances realizes this, perhaps; and she may never realize it, with luck. The type of man who is tapped for Bones is rarely also tapped for bed; but with a lovely girl like Frances intention counts as much as performance.

So, anyhow, they all sleep well and where did the money come from that they're all so happy with and use so well and gracefully? The money came from selling something everybody uses by the millions of bottles, which costs three cents a quart to make, for a dollar a bottle in the large (pint) size, fifty cents in the medium, and a quarter in the small. But it's more economical to buy the large, and if you make ten dollars a week the cost is just the same to you as though you were a millionaire, and the product's really good. It does just what it says it will and more besides. Grateful users from all over the world keep writing in discovering new uses and old users are as loyal to it as Harold Tompkins, the fiancé, is to Skull and Bones or Stanley Baldwin is to Harrow. There are no suicides when money's made that way and every one sleeps soundly on the yacht *Alzira III,* master Jon Jacobson, crew of fourteen, owner and family aboard.

At pier four there is a 34-foot yawl-rigged yacht with two of the three hundred and twenty-four Esthonians who are sailing around in different parts of the world, in boats between 28 and 36 feet long and sending back articles to the Esthonian newspapers. These articles are very popular in Esthonia and bring their authors between a dollar and a dollar and thirty cents a column. They take the place occupied by the baseball or football news in American newspapers and are run under the heading of Sagas of Our Intrepid

Voyagers. No well-run yacht basin in Southern waters is complete without at least two sunburned, salt bleached-headed Esthonians who are waiting for a check from their last article. When it comes they will sail to another yacht basin and write another saga. They are very happy too. Almost as happy as the people on the *Alzira III*. It's great to be an Intrepid Voyager.

On the *Irydia IV*, a professional son-in-law of the very rich and his mistress, named Dorothy, the wife of that highly paid Hollywood director, John Hollis, whose brain is in the process of outlasting his liver so that he will end up calling himself a Communist, to save his soul, his other organs being too corroded to attempt to save them, are asleep. The son-in-law, big-framed, good looking in a poster way, lies on his back snoring, but Dorothy Hollis, the director's wife, is awake and she puts on a dressing gown and, going out onto the deck, looks across the dark water of the yacht basin to the line the breakwater makes. It is cool on the deck and the wind blows her hair and she smooths it back from her tanned forehead, and pulling the robe tighter around her, her nipples rising in the cold, notices the lights of a boat coming along the outside of the breakwater. She watches them moving steadily and rapidly along and then at the entrance to the basin the boat's searchlight is switched on and comes across the water in a sweep that blinds her as it passes, picking up the coast guard pier where it lit up the group of men waiting there and the shining black of the new ambulance from the funeral home which also doubles at funerals as a hearse.

I suppose it would be better to take some luminol, Dorothy thought. I must get some sleep. Poor Eddie's tight as a tick. It means so much to him and he's so nice, but he gets so tight he goes right off to sleep. He's so sweet. Of course if I married him he'd be off with some one else, I suppose. He is sweet, though. Poor darling, he's so tight. I hope he won't feel miserable in the morning. I must go and set this wave and get some sleep. It looks like the devil. I do want to look lovely for him. He is sweet. I wish I'd brought a maid. I couldn't though. Not even Bates. I wonder how poor John is. Oh, he's sweet too. I hope he's better. His poor liver. I wish I were there to look after him. I might go and get some sleep so I won't look a fright tomorrow. Eddie is sweet. So's John and his poor liver. Oh, his poor liver. Eddie is sweet. I wish he hadn't gotten so tight. He's so big and jolly and marvellous and all. Perhaps he won't get so tight tomorrow.

She went below and found her way to her cabin, and sitting before the mirror commenced brushing her hair a hundred strokes. She smiled at herself in the mirror as the long bristled brush swept through her lovely hair. Eddie is sweet. Yes, he is. I wish he hadn't gotten so tight. Men all have something that way. Look at John's liver. Of course you can't look at it. It must look dreadful really. I'm glad you can't see it. Nothing about a man's really ugly though. It's funny how they think it is though. I suppose a liver though. Or kidneys. Kidneys en brochette. How many kidneys are there? There's two of nearly everything except stomach and heart. And brain of course. There. That's a hundred strokes. I love to brush my hair. It's almost the only thing you do that's good for you that's fun. I mean by yourself. Oh, Eddie is sweet. Suppose I just went in there. No, he is too tight. Poor boy. I'll take the luminol.

She looked at herself in the mirror. She was extraordinarily pretty, with a small, very fine figure. Oh, I'll do, she thought. Some of it isn't as good as some of the rest of it, but I'll do for a while yet. You do have to have sleep though. I love to sleep. I wish I could get just one good natural real sleep the way we slept when we were kids. I suppose that's the thing about growing up and marrying and having children and then drinking too much and then doing all the things you shouldn't. If you could sleep well I don't think any of it would be bad for you. Except drinking too much I suppose. Poor John and his liver and Eddie. Eddie is darling, anyway. He is cute. I'd better take the luminol.

She made a face at herself in the glass.

"You'd better take the luminol," she said in a whisper. She took the luminol with a glass of water from the chronium-plated thermos carafe that was on the locker by the bed.

It makes you nervous, she thought. But you have to sleep. I wonder how Eddie would be if we were married. He would be running around with some one younger I suppose. I suppose they can't help the way they're built any more than we can. I just want a lot of it and I feel so fine, and being some one else or some one new doesn't really mean a thing. It's just it itself, and you would love them always if they gave it to you. The same one I mean. But they aren't built that way. They want some one new, or some one younger, or some one that they shouldn't have, or some one that looks like some one else. Or if you're dark they want a blonde. Or if you're blonde they go for a redhead. Or if you're a redhead then it's something else. A Jewish girl I guess, and if they've had really enough they want Chinese or Lesbians or goodness knows what. I don't know. Or they just get tired, I suppose. You can't blame them if that's the way they are and I can't help John's liver either or that he's drunk so much he isn't any good. He was good. He was marvellous. He was. He really was. And Eddie is. But now he's tight. I suppose I'll end up a bitch. Maybe I'm one now. I suppose you never know when you get to be one. Only her best friends would tell her. You don't read it in Mr. Winchell. That would be a good new thing for him to announce. Bitch-hood. Mrs. John Hollis canined into town from the coast. Better than babies. More common I guess. But women have a bad time really.

The better you treat a man and the more you show
him you love him the quicker he gets tired of you. I
suppose the good ones are made to have a lot of wives
but it's awfully wearing trying to be a lot of wives
yourself, and then some one simple takes him when
he's tired of that. I suppose we all end up as bitches
but who's fault is it? The bitches have the most fun
but you have to be awfully stupid really to be a
good one. Like Helène Bradley. Stupid and well-
intentioned and really selfish to be a good one. Probably I'm one already. They say you can't tell and that
you always think you're not. There must be men who
don't get tired of you or of it. There must be. But
who has them? The ones we know are all brought up
wrong. Let's not go into that now. No, not into that.
Nor back to all those cars and all those dances. I wish
that luminol would work. Damn Eddie, really. He
shouldn't have really gotten so tight. It isn't fair,
really. No one can help the way they're built but
getting tight has nothing to do with that. I suppose
I am a bitch all right, but if I lie here now all night
and can't sleep I'll go crazy and if I take too much
of that damned stuff I'll feel awfully all day tomorrow and then sometimes it won't put you to sleep and
anyway I'll be cross and nervous and feel frightful.
Oh, well, I might as well. I hate to but what can
you do? What can you do but go ahead and do it
even though, even though, even anyway, oh, he *is*
sweet, no he isn't, I'm sweet, yes you are, you're

lovely, oh, you're so lovely, yes, lovely, and I didn't want to, but I am, now I am really, he *is* sweet, no he's not, he's not even here, I'm here, I'm always here and I'm the one that cannot go away, no, never. You sweet one. You lovely. Yes you are. You lovely, lovely, lovely. Oh, yes, lovely. And you're me. So that's it. So that's the way it is. So what about it always now and over now. All over now. All right. I don't care. What difference does it make? It isn't wrong if I don't feel badly. And I don't. I just feel sleepy now and if I wake I'll do it again before I'm really awake.

She went to sleep then, remembering, just before she was finally asleep, to turn on her side so that her face did not rest on the pillow. She remembered, no matter how sleepy, how terribly bad it is for the face to sleep that way, resting on the pillow.

There were two other yachts in the harbor but every one was asleep on them, too, when the Coast Guard boat towed Freddy Wallace's boat, the *Queen Conch,* into the dark yacht basin and tied up along-side the Coast Guard pier.

CHAPTER TWENTY-FIVE

HARRY MORGAN knew nothing about it when they handed a stretcher down from the pier, and, with two men holding it on the deck of the gray-painted cutter under a floodlight outside the captain's cabin, two others picked him up from the captain's bunk and moved unsteadily out to ease him onto the stretcher. He had been unconscious since the early evening and his big body sagged the canvas of the stretcher deeply as the four men lifted it up toward the pier.

"Up with it now."

"Hold his legs. Don't let him slip."

"Up with it."

They got the stretcher onto the pier.

"How is he, Doctor?" asked the sheriff as the men shoved the stretcher into the ambulance.

"He's alive," said the doctor. "That's all you can say."

"He's been out of his head or unconscious ever since we picked him up," the boatswain's mate commanding the Coast Guard cutter said. He was a short chunky man with glasses that shone in the floodlight. He needed a shave. "All your Cuban stiffs are back in the launch. We left everything like it was. We didn't touch anything. We just put the two down that might have gone overboard. Everything's just like it was. The money and the guns. Everything."

"Come on," said the sheriff. "Can you run a flood-light back there?"

"I'll have them plug one in on the dock," the dockmaster said. He went off to get the light and the cord.

"Come on," said the sheriff. They went astern with flashlights. "I want you to show me exactly how you found them. Where's the money?"

"In those two bags."

"How much is there?"

"I don't know. I opened one up and saw it was the money and shut it up. I didn't want to touch it."

"That's right," said the sheriff. "That's exactly right."

"Everything's just like it was except we put two of the stiffs off the tanks down into the cockpit so they wouldn't roll overboard, and we carried that big ox of a Harry aboard and put him in my bunk. I figured him to pass out before we got him in. He's in a hell of a shape."

"He's been unconscious all the time?"

"He was out of his head at first," said the skipper. "But you couldn't make out what he was saying. We listened to a lot of it but it didn't make sense. Then he got unconscious. There's your layout. Just like it

was only that niggery looking one on his side is laying where Harry lay. He was on the bench over the
starboard tank hanging over the coaming and the
other dark one by the side of him was on the other
bench, the port side, hunched over on his face. Watch
out. Don't light any matches. She's full of gas."

"There ought to be another body," said the sheriff.

"That's all there was. The money's in that bag.
The guns are right where they were."

"We better have somebody from the bank to see
the money opened," said the sheriff.

"O.K.," said the skipper. "That's a good idea."

"We can take the bag to my office and seal it."

"That's a good idea," said the skipper.

Under the floodlight the green and white of the
launch had a freshly shiny look. This came from the
dew on her deck and on the top of the house. The
splinterings showed fresh through her white paint.
Astern of her the water was a clear green under the
light and there were small fish about the pilings.

In the cockpit the inflated faces of the dead men
were shiny under the light, lacquered brown where
the blood had dried. There were empty .45 caliber
shells in the cockpit around the dead and the
Thompson gun lay in the stern where Harry had put
it down. The two leather briefcases the men had
brought the money aboard in, leaned against one of
the gas tanks.

"I thought maybe I ought to take the money on

board while we were towing her," the skipper said.
"Then I thought it was better to leave it just exactly
like it was so long as the weather was light."

"It was right to leave it," the sheriff said. "What's
become of the other man, Albert Tracy, the fisherman?"

"I don't know. This is just how it was except for
shifting those two," the skipper said. "They're all
shot to pieces except that one there under the wheel
laying on his back. He's just shot in the back of the
head. It come out through the front. You can see
what it did."

"He's the one that looked like a kid," the sheriff
said.

"He don't look like anything now," the skipper
said.

"That big one there is the one had the submachine
gun and who killed attorney Robert Simmons," the
sheriff said. "What do you suppose happened? How
the devil did they all get shot?"

"They must have got fighting among themselves,"
the skipper said. "They must have had a dispute on
how to split the money."

"We'll cover them up until morning," the sheriff
said. "I'll take those bags."

Then, as they were standing there in the cockpit, a
woman came running up the pier past the Coast
Guard cutter, and behind her came the crowd. The
woman was gaunt, middle-aged and bare-headed, and

her stringy hair had come undone and was down on her neck although it was still knotted at the end. As she saw the bodies in the cockpit she commenced to scream. She stood on the pier screaming with her head back while two other women held her arms. The crowd, which had come close behind her, formed around her, jostled close, looking down at the launch.

"God damn it," said the sheriff. "Who left that gate open? Get something to cover those bodies; blankets, sheets, anything, and we'll get this crowd out of here."

The woman stopped screaming and looked down into the launch, then put back her head and screamed again.

"Where they got him?" said one of the women near her.

"Where they put Albert?"

The woman who was screaming stopped it and looked in the launch again.

"He ain't there," she said. "Hey, you, Roger Johnson," she shouted at the sheriff. "Where's Albert? Where's Albert?"

"He isn't on board, Mrs. Tracy," the sheriff said. The woman put her head back and screamed again, the chords in her scrawny throat rigid, her hands clenched, her hair shaking.

In the back of the crowd people were shoving and elbowing to get to the dock side.

"Come on. Let somebody else see."

"They're going to cover them up."

And in Spanish, "Let me pass. Let me look. *Hay cuatro muertos. Todos son muertos.* Let me see."

Now the woman was screaming, "Albert! Albert! Oh, my God, where's Albert?"

In the back of the crowd two young Cubans who had just come up and who could not penetrate the crowd stepped back, then ran and shoved forward together. The front line of the crowd swayed and bulged, then, in the middle of a scream, Mrs. Tracy and her two supporters toppled, hung slanted forward in desperate unbalance and then, while the supporters wildly hung to safety, Mrs. Tracy, still screaming, fell into the green water, the scream becoming a splash and bubble.

Two Coast Guard men dove into the clear green water where Mrs. Tracy was splashing in the floodlight. The sheriff leaned out on the stern and shoved a boat hook out to her and finally, raised from below by the two Coast Guardsmen, pulled up by the arms by the sheriff, she was hoisted onto the stern of the launch. No one in the crowd had made a move to aid her, and, as she stood dripping on the stern, she looked up at them, shook both her fists at them and shouted, "Basards! Bishes!" Then as she looked into the cockpit she wailed, "Alber. Whersh Alber?"

"He's not on board, Mrs. Tracy," the sheriff said, taking up a blanket to put around her. "Try to be calm, Mrs. Tracy. Try to be brave."

"My plate," said Mrs. Tracy tragically. "Losht my plate."

"We'll dive it up in the morning," the skipper of the Coast Guard cutter told her. "We'll get it all right."

The Coast Guard men had climbed up on the stern and were standing dripping. "Come on. Let's go," one of them said. "I'm getting cold."

"Are you all right, Mrs. Tracy?" the sheriff said, putting the blanket around her.

"All rie?" said Mrs. Tracy. "All rie?" then clenched both her hands and put her head back to really scream. Mrs. Tracy's grief was greater than she could bear.

The crowd listened to her and was silent and respectful. Mrs. Tracy provided just the sound effect that was needed to go with the sight of the dead bandits that were now being covered with Coast Guard blankets by the sheriff and one of the deputies, thus veiling the greatest sight the town had seen since the Isleño had been lynched, years before, out on the County Road and then hung up to swing from a telephone pole in the lights of all the cars that had come out to see it.

The crowd was disappointed when the bodies were covered but they alone of all the town had seen them. They had seen Mrs. Tracy fall into the water and they had, before they came in, seen Harry Morgan carried on a stretcher into the Marine Hospital. When

the sheriff ordered them out of the yacht basin they
went quietly and happily. They knew how privileged
they had been.

Meanwhile at the Marine Hospital Harry Morgan's wife, Marie, and her three daughters waited on
a bench in the receiving room. The three girls were
crying and Marie was biting on a handkerchief. She
hadn't been able to cry since about noon.

"Daddy's shot in the stomach," one of the girls said
to her sister.

"It's terrible," said the sister.

"Be quiet," said the older sister. "I'm praying for
him. Don't interrupt me."

Marie said nothing and only sat there, biting on a
handkerchief and on her lower lip.

After a while the doctor came out. She looked at
him and he shook his head.

"Can I go in?" she asked.

"Not yet," he said. She went over to him. "Is he
gone?" she said.

"I'm afraid so, Mrs. Morgan."

"Can I go in and see him?"

"Not yet. He's in the operating room."

"Oh, Christ," said Marie. "Oh, Christ. I'll take the
girls home. Then I'll be back."

Her throat suddenly was swollen hard and shut so
she could not swallow.

"Come on, you girls," she said. The three girls

followed her out to the old car where she got into the driver's seat and started the engine.

"How's Daddy?" one of the girls asked.

Marie did not answer.

"How's Daddy, Mother?"

"Don't talk to me," Marie said. "Just don't talk to me."

"But——"

"Shut up, Honey," said Marie. "Just shut up and pray for him." The girls began to cry again.

"Damn it," said Marie. "Don't cry like that. I said pray for him."

"We will," said one of the girls. "I haven't stopped since we were at the hospital."

As they turned onto the worn white coral of the Rocky Road the headlight of the car showed a man walking unsteadily along ahead of them.

"Some poor rummy," thought Marie. "Some poor goddamned rummy."

They passed the man, who had blood on his face, and who kept on unsteadily in the dark after the lights of the car had gone on up the street. It was Richard Gordon on his way home.

At the door of the house Marie stopped the car.

"Go to bed, you girls," she said. "Go on up to bed."

"But what about Daddy?" one of the girls asked.

"Don't you talk to me," Marie said. "For Christ sake, please don't speak to me."

She turned the car in the road and started back toward the hospital.

Back at the hospital Marie Morgan climbed the steps in a rush. The doctor met her on the porch as he came out through the screen door. He was tired and on his way home.

"He's gone, Mrs. Morgan," he said.

"He's dead?"

"He died on the table."

"Can I see him?"

"Yes," the doctor said. "He went very peacefully, Mrs. Morgan. He was in no pain."

"Oh, hell," said Marie. Tears began to run down her cheeks. "Oh," she said. "Oh, oh, oh."

The doctor put his hand on her shoulder.

"Don't touch me," Marie said. Then, "I want to see him."

"Come on," the doctor said. He walked with her down a corridor and into the white room where Harry Morgan lay on a wheeled table, a sheet over his great body. The light was very bright and cast no shadows. Marie stood in the doorway looking terrified by the light.

"He didn't suffer at all, Mrs. Morgan," the doctor said. Marie did not seem to hear him.

"Oh, Christ," she said, and began to cry again. "Look at his goddamned face."

CHAPTER TWENTY-SIX

I DON'T know, Marie Morgan was thinking, sitting at the dining-room table. I can take it just a day at a time and a night at a time, and maybe it gets different. It's the goddamned nights. If I cared about those girls it would be different. But I don't care about those girls. I've got to do something about them though. I've got to get started on something. Maybe you get over being dead inside. I guess it don't make any difference. I got to start to do something anyway. It's been a week today. I'm afraid if I think about him on purpose I'll get so I can't remember how he looks. That was when I got that awful panic when I couldn't remember his face. I got to get started doing something no matter how I feel. If he'd have left some money or if there'd been rewards it would have been better but I wouldn't feel no better. First thing I've got to do is try to sell the house. The bastards that shot him. Oh, the dirty bastards. That's the only feeling I got. Hate and a hollow feeling. I'm empty like a empty house. Well, I got to start to do something. I should have gone to the funeral. But I couldn't go. I got to start to do something now though. Ain't nobody going to come back any more when they're dead.

Him, like he was, snotty and strong and quick, and like some kind of expensive animal. It would always get me just to watch him move. I was so lucky all that time to have him. His luck went bad first in Cuba. Then it kept right worse and worse until a Cuban killed him.

Cubans are bad luck for Conchs. Cubans are bad luck for anybody. They got too many niggers there too. I remember that time he took me over to Havana when he was making such good money and we were walking in the park and a nigger said something to me and Harry smacked him, and picked up his straw hat that fell off, and sailed it about a half a block and a taxi ran over it. I laughed so it made my belly ache.

That was the first time I ever made my hair blonde that time there in that beauty parlor on the Prado. They were working on it all afternoon and it was naturally so dark they didn't want to do it and I was afraid I'd look terrible, but I kept telling them to see if they couldn't make it a little lighter, and the man would go over it with that orange wood stick with cotton on the end, dipping it in that bowl that had the stuff in it sort of smoky like the way it steamed sort of, and the comb; parting the strands with one end of the stick and the comb and going over them and letting it dry and I was sitting there scared inside my chest of what I was having done and all I'd say was, just see if you can't make it a little lighter.

And finally he said, that's just as light as I can make it safely, Madame, and then he shampooed it, and put a wave in, and I was afraid to look even for fear it would be terrible, and he waved it parted on one side and high behind my ears with little tight curls in back, and it still wet I couldn't tell how it looked except it looked all changed and I looked strange to myself. And he put a net over it wet and put me under the dryer and all the time I was scared about it. And then when I come out from under the dryer he took the net off and the pins out and combed it out and it was just like gold.

And I came out of the place and saw myself in the mirror and it shone so in the sun and was so soft and silky when I put my hand and touched it, and I couldn't believe it was me and I was so excited I was choked with it.

I walked down the Prado to the café where Harry was waiting and I was so excited feeling all funny inside, sort of faint like, and he stood up when he saw me coming and he couldn't take his eyes off me and his voice was thick and funny when he said, "Jesus, Marie, you're beautiful."

And I said, "You like me blonde?"

"Don't talk about it," he said. "Let's go to the hotel."

And I said, "O.K., then. Let's go." I was twenty-six then.

And that's how he always was with me and that's the way I always was about him. He said he never had anything like me and I know there wasn't any men like him. I know it too damned well and now he's dead.

Now I got to get started on something. I know I got to. But when you got a man like that and some lousy Cuban shoots him you can't just start right out; because everything inside of you is gone. I don't know what to do. It ain't like when he was away on trips. Then he was always coming back but now I got to go on the rest of my life. And I'm big now and ugly and old and he ain't here to tell me that I ain't. I'd have to hire a man to do it now I guess and then I wouldn't want him. So that's the way it goes. That's the way it goes all right.

And he was so goddamned good to me and reliable too, and he always made money some way and I never had to worry about money, only about him, and now that's all gone.

It ain't what happens to the one gets killed. I wouldn't mind if it was me got killed. With Harry at the end there he was just tired, the doctor said. He never woke up even. I was glad he died easy because Jesus Christ he must have suffered in that boat. I wonder if he thought about me or what he thought about. I guess like that you don't think about anybody. I guess it must have hurt too bad. But finally he was just too tired. I wish to Christ it was me was dead. But that ain't any good to wish. Nothing is any good to wish.

I couldn't go to the funeral. But people don't understand that. They don't know how you feel. Because good men are scarce. They just don't have them. Nobody knows the way you feel, because they don't know what it's all about that way. I know. I know too well. And if I live now twenty years what am I going to do? Nobody's going to tell me that and there ain't nothing now but take it every day the way it comes and just get started doing something right away. That's what I got to do. But Jesus Christ, what do you do at nights is what I want to know.

How do you get through nights if you can't sleep? I guess you find out like you find out how it feels to lose your husband. I guess you find out all right. I guess you find out everything in this goddamned life. I guess you do all right. I guess I'm probably finding out right now. You just go dead inside and everything is easy. You just get dead like most people are most of the time. I guess that's how it is all right. I guess that's just about what happens to you. Well, I've got a good start. I've got a good start if that's what you have to do. I guess that's what you have to do all right. I guess that's it. I guess that's what it comes to. All right. I got a good start then. I'm way ahead of everybody now.

Outside it was a lovely, cool, sub-tropical winter

day and the palm branches were sawing in the light north wind. Some winter people rode by the house on bicycles. They were laughing. In the big yard of the house across the street a peacock squawked.

Through the window you could see the sea looking hard and new and blue in the winter light.

A large white yacht was coming into the harbor and seven miles out on the horizon you could see a tanker, small and neat in profile against the blue sea, hugging the reef as she made to the westward to keep from wasting fuel against the stream.

ABOUT THE AUTHOR

Ernest Hemingway was born in Oak Park, Illinois, in 1899, and began his writing career with *The Kansas City Star* in 1917. During the First World War he volunteered as an ambulance driver on the Italian front but was invalided home, having been seriously wounded while serving with the Red Cross. In 1921 Hemingway settled in Paris, where he became part of the expatriate circle of Gertrude Stein, F. Scott Fitzgerald, Ezra Pound, and Ford Madox Ford. His first book, *Three Stories and Ten Poems,* was published in Paris in 1923 and was followed by the short story collection *In Our Time,* which marked his American debut in 1925. With the appearance of *The Sun Also Rises* in 1926, Hemingway became not only the voice of the "lost generation" but the preeminent writer of his time. This was followed by *Men Without Women* in 1927, when Hemingway returned to the United States, and his novel of the Italian front, *A Farewell to Arms* (1929). In the 1930s, Hemingway settled in Key West, and later in Cuba, but he traveled widely—to Spain, Italy, and Africa—and wrote about his experiences in *Death in the Afternoon* (1932), his classic treatise on bullfighting, and *Green Hills of Africa* (1935), an account of big-game hunting in Africa. Later he reported on the Spanish Civil War, which became the background for his brilliant war novel, *For Whom the Bell Tolls* (1940), hunted U-boats in the Caribbean, and covered the European front during the Second World War. Hemingway's most popular work, *The Old Man and the Sea* (1952), was awarded the Pulitzer Prize in 1953, and in 1954 Hemingway won the Nobel Prize in Literature "for his powerful, style-forming mastery of the art of narration." One of the most important influences on the development of the short story and novel in American fiction, Hemingway has seized the imagination of the American public like no other twentieth-century author. He died, by suicide, in Ketchum, Idaho, in 1961. His other works include *The Torrents of Spring* (1926), *Winner Take Nothing* (1933), *To Have and Have Not* (1937), *The Fifth Column and the First Forty-nine Stories* (1938), *Across the River and Into the Trees* (1950), and posthumously, *A Moveable Feast* (1964), *Islands in the Stream* (1970), *The Dangerous Summer* (1985), and *The Garden of Eden* (1986).